D0092170

WSP

# THE UNEXPLAINABLE
# DISAPPEARANCE OF
# MARS
# PATEL

# SHEELA CHARI

Based on the podcast series created by
**BENJAMIN STROUSE**
**CHRIS TARRY**
**DAVID KREIZMAN**
**JENNY TURNER HALL**

**WALKER BOOKS**

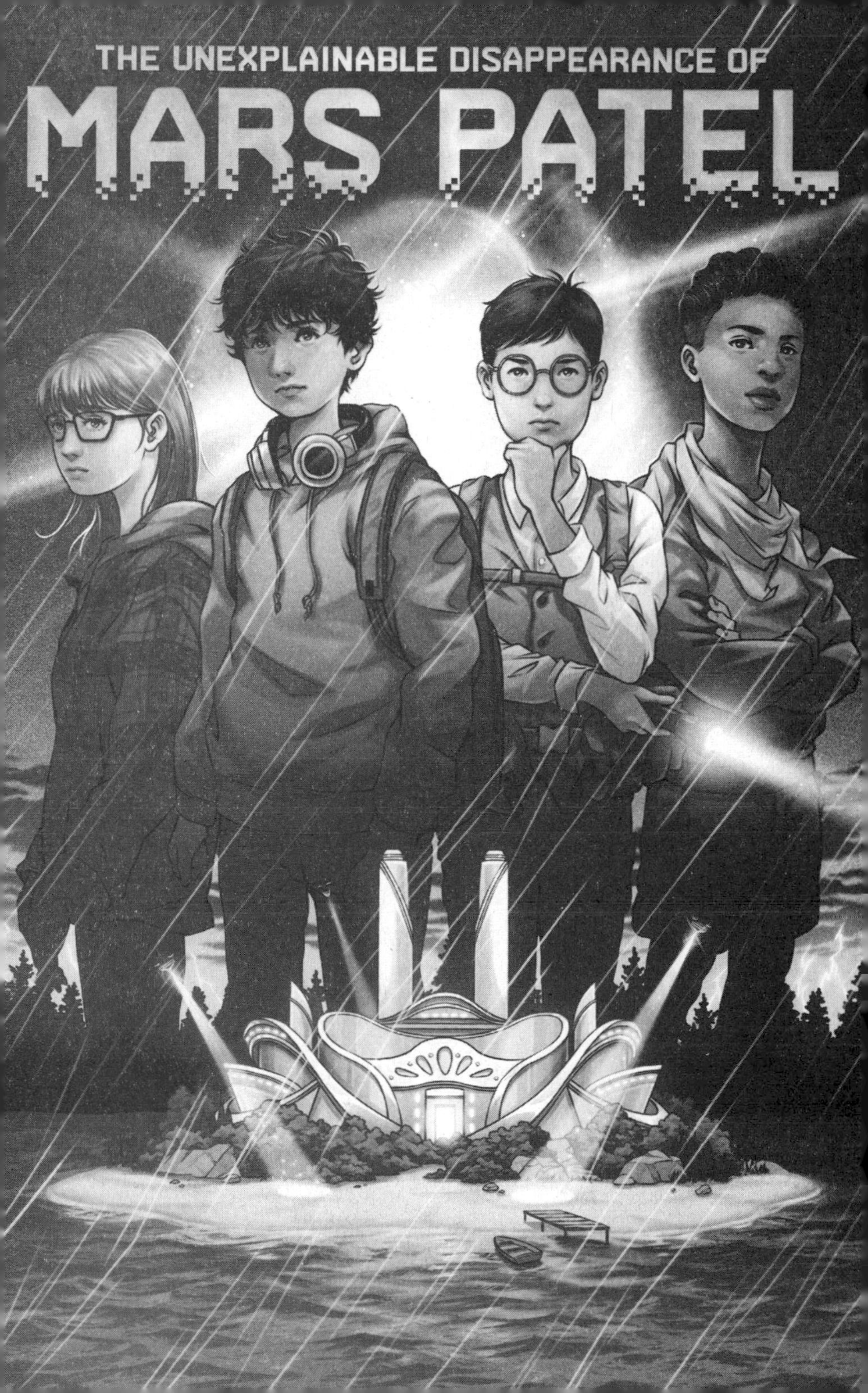
THE UNEXPLAINABLE DISAPPEARANCE OF
MARS PATEL

This
is a
work of
f i c t i o n .
Names, char-
acters, places,
and incidents are
either products of
the author's imagina-
tion or, if real, are used
fictitiously. • Text copyright
© 2020 by Mars Patel • Pub-
lished by arrangement with Mars
Patel LLC • All rights reserved. No part
of this book may be reproduced, trans-
mitted, or stored in an information retrieval
system in any form or by any means, graphic,
electronic, or mechanical, including photocopying,
taping, and recording, without prior written permission from the publisher. • First paperback edition 2021 •
Library of Congress Catalog Card Number 2020918839 •
ISBN 978-1-5362-0956-3 (hardcover) • ISBN 978-1-5362-
1910-4 (paperback) • This book was typeset in Utopia. • Walker
Books US • a division of Candlewick Press • 99 Dover Street •
Somerville, Massachusetts 02144 • www.walkerbooksus.com •
Printed in Eagan, MN, USA • 21 22 23 24 25 26 TRC 10 9 8 7 6 5 4 3 2 1

W08

FOR MEERA

Hey there! Yeah, you!

Are you searching for adventure?

Will it be you leading the way someday?

You may not know it,

but someday is sooner than you think.

Something BIG is happening soon.

To the stars!

# 1
# AURORA?

Wed, Oct 14, 2:46 pm

Mars

guys I got 5 more days of detention from Baker

Caddie

rly??

Mars

she's mad cuz I set her desk on fire

JP

oof

Mars

potassium ignites with hydrogen who knew

Toothpick

it's called an exothermic reaction

Mars

now you tell me

**Aurora**
detention is the WORSTTTT

**Toothpick**
actually global warming is—more bodily harm

**Caddie**
ugh Mr. Q is bringing cookies AGAIN

**Jonas**
dude detention's bad enough
my stomach can't take another one of his cookies

**Aurora**
I'm so done with this school

**Mars**
Lol is that why u missed English today

**Aurora**
time for action

**Mars**
like what

**Mars**
Aurora?

**Mars · Caddie · JP · Jonas · Toothpick · Aurora**

Thurs, Oct 15, 2:49 pm

**Mars**
anyone see Aurora

**Jonas**
prob skipped

2

## Mars · Caddie · JP · Jonas · Toothpick · Aurora

Sun, Oct 18, 7:50 pm

**JP**
I lost my math homework someone helpppp

**Caddie**
u can copy off me

**JP**
thx owe u

**Mars**
where's Aurora

**Toothpick**
Maybe she's sick

**Jonas**
or out of town

## Mars · Aurora

Sun, Oct 18, 8:00 pm

**Mars**
r u there

Sun, Oct 18, 10:35 pm

**Mars**
pls write back

Sun, Oct 18, 11:58 pm

**Mars**
Aurora??

3

# 2
## CODE RED

On his way to school Monday morning, Mars kept checking his phone for messages.

So far, nothing. Where was Aurora? Why hadn't she written back? As he reached the front entrance of the school, a voice called from behind.

"Mars! Wait up!"

He turned and saw Caddie coming up the sidewalk. Her hair was tucked inside her flannel jacket, and her glasses were foggy from the early-morning mist.

She saw his headphones. "Podcast?"

Mars slipped them off and hung them around his neck. "Yeah," he said.

Every morning he listened to Oliver Pruitt's podcast on his way to school. It helped him think. Sometimes it gave him ideas, and he could use a good one now.

"Did you hear from Aurora?" he asked.

Caddie shook her head, watching him carefully. "You're worried, aren't you?"

Mars grimaced. "You're not doing that thing where you're in my head? 'Cause you know I hate that." For as long as he could remember, Caddie had the ability to sense what he was feeling. She could do it with all their friends except Aurora. Aurora was different. She was good at blocking out the world. But apparently Mars was an open book.

"I'm not doing anything, honest," Caddie said quickly.

"Well, it sure feels like you're in my head."

"I don't need to be," she said. "It's right there on your face."

"She hasn't responded to any of my texts."

"Don't worry," Caddie said. "You know how she is. She's probably caught up in some Aurora thing." They continued walking as kids jostled past from the school bus parked behind them. "So what's he saying now?"

"Who?"

"Oliver Pruitt. You know, the podcast. You were listening to it just now."

"Oh, yeah." Mars hesitated. It was always hard to explain Oliver Pruitt to anyone, even Caddie. Like, how did he describe that strange feeling he got in his throat every time he heard this man he'd never met in his life speak? "Um, he says something BIG is going to happen," he said.

"Really? Like what?"

Mars thought about what Oliver had said this morning. *Something BIG is happening soon.* It wasn't the words but how he'd said them, like Oliver had been bursting at the seams. Was it a good big thing? Mars didn't know. "Not sure," he said. "Just something big."

Caddie had stopped talking because they'd entered the school. All the students together in the hall had a way of overwhelming her. Mars called it system overload. Whatever it was, it always took Caddie a minute to adjust to everyone's thoughts crowding around her. By the time they got to their lockers, Caddie was better. But Mars wasn't. He was still thinking about Aurora.

"Five days," he announced, throwing his coat and backpack into his locker, where it hit a small poster of Oliver Pruitt taped to the back.

Jonas was standing at his locker already, wearing his Mariners baseball cap.

"Five what?" he asked distractedly. He was playing Astro Surf on his phone.

"Five days since Aurora disappeared," Mars said impatiently. "Don't you remember?"

Caddie nodded. "Five days is kinda long, even for Aurora."

"What does that mean?" Mars asked.

"Dude, Aurora skips all the time," Jonas said.

*But not without telling me,* Mars thought. Aurora might

be secretive with other people, but she'd always trusted him.

"Out of my way, Martian Patel," said Clyde Boofsky, barreling through the hall. As H. G. Wells's only sixth grader to bench-press a hundred pounds, the Boof was made of steel.

"Watch where you're going, Boof," Mars said. "Though you probably need GPS to find your turd-size brain."

Clyde flipped his finger at Mars and kept walking.

"Why does he never bother you?" Mars asked Jonas.

Jonas shrugged. "Because he knows I'd kick his butt."

It was true. Clyde might have been strong, but Jonas towered a good three inches over him.

Mars sighed—he hated being the shortest boy in sixth grade.

Meanwhile, Caddie was frowning and holding two fingertips to her temple.

"What's the matter, Caddie? Are you OK?" Mars asked.

She shook her head, wincing. "Ow. I'm getting one of those headaches."

Lately, Caddie's headaches had turned into warning signs. They used to come for small things, like the one she'd got right before Mars slipped in the cafeteria, or Toothpick got hit in the head with a flying sandwich. But then they'd come for more serious stuff. Like before her brother twisted his ankle in gym, or when her dad lost his job. Each time, there was a quick throb at her temples.

Suddenly a siren blared through the school, echoing down the halls.

"Attention, attention, students and faculty. This is a Code Red. Please remain calm and proceed with lockdown protocol." The announcement came over the PA.

They all looked at one another. Was it a drill? The first-period bell hadn't even rung.

The PA repeated. "This a Code Red. Please proceed with lockdown protocol."

Around them students started running while teachers called out. Everyone knew what a Code Red was. Every month they had to do the drills. They hid under desks or inside classroom closets, and kids would whisper until it was over. Jonas always managed to sneak in his phone and would zone out on his games.

Not Mars. Each time there was a drill, he'd wonder if the dangerous thing he always expected to happen was finally happening, and life would never be the same. His life had changed on a dime before. It could happen again.

"We repeat. This is a Code Red. Please proceed with lockdown protocol."

"Is this for real?" Jonas asked them.

For a moment Mars remembered the podcast. Was *this* the big thing Oliver Pruitt had said was going to happen?

"Caddie would know," he said. He whirled around. "Right, Caddie?"

Caddie's face was awash in pain. The siren continued to blare.

"Ow!" She clutched her head. "This is real, guys. This is real!"

# H. G. Wells Middle School

---

## PROCEDURE FOR CODE RED ALERT

A CODE RED alert is used when there is an *immediate* and *imminent* threat to the school.

Remember: **"Don't Be Scared, Be Prepared"**

### PRINCIPAL'S PROTOCOL:

- Make announcement over PA: "This is a Code Red." (repeat 3x)
- Call 911
- Report to the nearest classroom immediately

### TEACHERS' PROTOCOL:

Check hallways for students. Once all students are in the classrooms:

- Secure doors
- Turn out lights
- Cover windows
- Hide
- No talking!
- Do not open doors for ANYONE
- Take attendance
- Check email and monitors for updates and when to evacuate if necessary

**During CODE RED, do not hide in bathrooms, alcoves, or hallway closets.**

# 3
## ON THE OTHER SIDE

**H**urry," Mars told them. "You know where."

Caddie didn't need to be reminded. While the rest of the students at H. G. Wells were sheltering in classrooms, they were heading someplace else. Most of the time the janitor closet was a storage room for mops and cleaning supplies. But it was also their secret meeting place. Aurora was the one who'd figured out that the janitor closet was the only place inside the school without a camera.

Caddie always worried they'd get caught. It was bad enough she kept getting sent to detention. Her mom would tell her how *she* never got into trouble when she was young—what was Caddie doing that was different? Was it because she was hanging out with Mars Patel?

But Aurora never seemed to care. In fact, she was always looking for ways to break the rules. Aurora said they should call themselves the MOPS: Mars's Opposition Party against School.

"Why do we need a name?" JP wanted to know. "And why against the school?"

"'Cause Mars is cool," Aurora said. "And this place sucks."

The MOPS idea didn't stick, but the closet did. It became the place they hid out during Hot Dog Field Day, pep rallies, or any time they didn't want to be seen in school. Aurora went whenever she felt like it (which was a lot). Sometimes she would drag Mars with her so they could plot their next prank. Once Caddie went to the closet on her own without telling Aurora. Epica Hernandez and her friends kept spiking the volleyball at Caddie in gym class until she had to skip, just to get away from Epica. She'd never admit it to Aurora, but it had felt good to escape that day.

When they reached the janitor closet, Caddie closed the door behind them. Then it was the three of them alone with the mops. In the dark.

"Ow!"

"Your headache, Caddie?"

"No, Jonas, your elbow!"

"Well, watch where you're sitting, Cads."

Caddie could hear the siren still going outside. Jonas's long limbs seemed to get in everyone's way, but finally he settled down, and so did Mars, though Caddie could feel him tense up next to her. It made her tense up, too.

"Ugh, my headache won't stop," she whispered.

"What are you seeing in your head?" Mars whispered back. "Is it about Aurora?"

"There he goes again about his girlfriend, Aurora," Jonas muttered.

"She isn't my girlfriend!"

"Right, you just talk about her all the time!"

"Jonas, you have to admit there's something weird about Aurora going dark for five days. No texts, nothing on Instagram. Nobody at home, nobody answering the phone."

Caddie sighed. Mars always got so defensive about Aurora. As far as he was concerned, Aurora could do no wrong. Not even when she forgot to call him or she teased him about Oliver Pruitt. That's how she was.

And that's how Mars was, too.

"Sometimes people go on vacation," Jonas said. "Like, remember when Aurora went to Vancouver without telling anyone?"

"That was just one weekend," Mars said. "And her great-aunt died."

"My family's tight, but we wouldn't go to a great-aunt's funeral," Jonas said. "I mean, what the heck is a great-aunt?"

"Look, Aurora's been missing for five days," Mars said,

"and now there's a Code Red in school. And Oliver Pruitt said—"

"Oh my god," Jonas said. "Why's it always about Aurora or Oliver Pruitt? Get a grip."

"I'm not making this stuff up," Mars said. "Oliver said on his podcast that something big was going to happen. And look—Code Red. Aurora gone. Something *is* happening, Jonas. I'm not sure what it is yet, but I *don't* think it's all a coincidence."

"Mars is right." Caddie rubbed her temples. The worst part about her headaches wasn't the pain but the feelings that came with them. Right now it felt like a great big blanket of worry was smothering her. "I'm scared, too. Like something bad is going to happen. But I can't see anything in my head, Mars. I feel it in my gut."

Jonas suddenly bent over. "Oh man, speaking of gut," he moaned. "I gotta go."

"You got to go where?" Mars asked.

"You know, like I gotta go!" Jonas stood up, almost knocking over a mop.

"Now?" Mars exclaimed. "You can't go out there. It's a Code Red. You heard what Caddie said. Something bad is going on."

"Yeah, but I gotta use the bathroom or it's going to be a Code Brown in my pants. I forgot to take my pills this morning." He reached for the doorknob.

"Jonas, don't!" Mars pleaded. "What if someone is out there?"

"I'm a big guy. I can handle it," Jonas said as he clutched his stomach. Jonas had been having digestive problems ever since he could remember. He'd probably visited every public bathroom in the Puget Sound area.

Caddie could sense Jonas's feelings bunching up inside him like they did whenever he felt sick. "He's right, Mars. He's, um, gotta go."

"And Caddie's never wrong," Jonas said. He opened the closet door and stepped out. "See you on the other side," he said, and shut the door behind him.

Then it was Mars and Caddie alone in the dark closet.

"I don't believe it," Mars whispered.

"I know. I hope he'll be OK." They sat in silence. "And I know you can't help worrying, Mars," she said. "You're worried about everyone. Even your dad."

He groaned. "Can you stop? Like, I'm not even aware of what I'm thinking, and there you are telling me all that." He paused. "And I'm not worrying about my dad, all right?"

"OK," Caddie said.

No one knew where Mars's dad was: not his mom, and certainly not Mars. The two of them had come to Port Elizabeth from India when Mars was little, and by then his dad was gone. Sometimes Mars got packages in the mail from him, like cookies or a book. Once he got a toy rocket on his birthday. Caddie knew Mars sometimes slept with it next to him, though he'd never told anyone. It was one of those things she sensed.

Outside the closet, it had grown strangely quiet. Was it just a drill? It was hard to tell.

"Do you think it's over?" Mars whispered.

Caddie wasn't sure. "My headache is getting better. Maybe it was just nerves."

"Let's wait a few more minutes, just in case," Mars said.

Caddie could feel him trying to sit quietly and not think any thoughts in case she sensed them. "It will be OK, Mars," she said gently.

He sighed. "Doing it again."

She cleared her throat. "Right, sorry." She shifted her weight, trying to pull her thoughts away from him. It's not that she *tried* to read his mind.

Caddie remembered the first time it had happened. They were in first grade, and she was crying (as usual). She cried a lot then. Most kids did when they fell down and scraped their knee. But Caddie cried because she could feel the teacher in class having mean thoughts. Genna couldn't do her addition tables. Gavin couldn't sit still. Lucy still wet her pants when she forgot to visit the bathroom after lunch. And Toothpick, he always knew the answers, and somehow that was a problem, too, for Mrs. Welt. Mrs.

Welt never said a word about how much she hated everyone for just being first graders, but Caddie *felt* it.

So she cried. She cried in class. She cried at recess. She cried at snacktime and lunch. Everyone called her a crybaby. Everyone but Mars. He would draw smiley faces on Post-it notes and leave them on her desk. He would save a swing for her on the playground. And one day when he sat next to Caddie during recess, she felt it. She felt his thoughts, which were *Caddie is a lot like me except I'm sad on the inside.* And then Caddie stopped crying.

Now Caddie never cried. She knew how to get along. But something had happened from that day in first grade when Mars stopped by at recess. She had always been good at telling what others were feeling, but with Mars it was different. It was like by feeling his thoughts, she'd become connected to him in some mysterious way that even she couldn't explain. And lately, there was something else, too, that confused her. Her feelings, which she'd never shared with him. But how often did you get stuck in a closet during a Code Red?

"So Mars, I know you might like Aurora and all," Caddie started slowly, "and I'm not reading your mind! I'm just saying that. But if you don't *like* like her, and since, well . . . the school dance is coming up, I thought . . ."

Just then an announcement came over the loudspeaker.

"Attention, students and faculty. Our lockdown is over. We have lifted the Code Red. Repeat: the lockdown is over. Please return to your classes."

Mars jumped up. "Code Red is over!"

Caddie got up, too. They blinked and stepped out from the dark closet into the brightly lit hall. Students were already passing them by on their way to class. Kids looked confused but relieved, too, and were already forgetting about the siren blaring a few minutes before. Now people were saying it had been a drill. Now teachers were telling students to get to class. Lockers were opening and shutting all around as the school lurched back to normal.

"I'm sorry, what were you saying, Caddie?" Mars asked. His curly hair was falling over his eyebrows in waves.

Caddie shook her head. "Nothing."

"OK. I'll go find Jonas," he said, and he was halfway down the hall. "See you later, Cads."

"In detention, right?" she called out to him.

🎧

*Something BIG is happening soon.* That's what Oliver Pruitt had said. Mars thought about that again as he walked down the hall to the boys' bathroom. Last week Oliver had predicted a hailstorm in Port Elizabeth, and the next day there were marble-size hailstones hitting Mars's apartment window. Oliver had said the San Bernardo Bridge would collapse, and it had, though luckily in the early morning, and no one got hurt. He had predicted weather patterns, traffic jams, stock market rallies, baseball wins, and government elections. It seemed like there was nothing that Oliver didn't know. And even though he was world-famous, his school, Pruitt Prep, was just a ferry ride away from Port Elizabeth, on Gale Island. That was what Mars marveled over the most. The *nearness*.

Of course, there was no chance of ever meeting Oliver Pruitt in real life. He also happened to be rich and famous, a billionaire inventor with his own line of electric cars, high-speed planes, and even space vehicles. In everything Mars had read about him or seen on YouTube, people said the same thing—how great Oliver was, like no one else in the world. He seemed both young and old, with a shock of dark hair, neatly shaved, impeccably dressed, with laugh lines around his gray eyes, and a faint, impatient smile that spoke of something humorous and disdainful at the same time. *To the stars*. That was his motto. Sometimes Mars found himself whispering those words under his breath. He whispered it to himself now: *To the stars*. What was the big thing that was going to happen? Because so far, Oliver had never been wrong.

By now Mars had reached the bathroom. "Jonas, you can come out. Code Red's done," he called, rapping on the door. There was no answer. Mars went inside. All the stalls were empty, the doors hanging wide open. "Jonas?"

From: messenger@hgwellsmiddleschool.org
To: Saira Patel <eyesontheprize@zapmail.com>
Date: Monday, October 19, 12:45 p.m.
Subject: Today's Code Red Lockdown

Dear Parents,

H. G. Wells was placed under a Code Red lockdown this morning. Port Elizabeth police officers were immediately dispatched to the building. At 8:23 a.m., the lockdown was lifted. Probable cause: a technical malfunction in our security system. As you know, our brand-new security software and surveillance equipment are state-of-the-art, and given to us through the generous support of an anonymous donor. *But rest assured that H. G. Wells Middle School is always ready to watch your children.*

All after-school activities will occur at their normal times, including detention.

Sincerely,
Dorena Fagan
Principal
H. G. Wells Middle School

## Ma · Mars

Ma

Mars! I get email from Principal Fagan. Code Red? Are you
ok??

Mars

I'm fine but Aurora and Jonas r missing!!!

Ma

What does the school say?

Mars

I tried to tell them but no one cares

Ma

Mars, stick to your own business. Don't get more
detention

Mars

What about Aurora and Jonas? Someone has to look for
them

Ma

That shouldn't be you. Promise me Mars

Mars

Nothing happened to me

Ma

Promise me you come straight home after detention
You have the GIFT test to study for

Ma

Mars?

Mon, Oct 19, 2:47 pm

Mars

**Now ur both missing?? Write back guys**

Mars

**Aurora? Jonas? Anyone?**

15 ▶ 30

Hey podcast listeners, Oliver Pruitt here.

How has your day been working out?

ANY SURPRISES?

At Pruitt Prep, I train students for surprises.

Not everyone is ready for the challenge.

But maybe you are.

Maybe you're a STAR IN THE MAKING.

But if you want to *get* here,

sometimes it means taking matters

into your own hands.

To the stars!

**360 Comments** ⊗

staryoda    45 min ago

**OP for prez guyz . . . like of the universe!!**

thisismars    37 min ago

**did the big thing happen—was that it??**

allie_j    33 min ago
OMG did something happen to you

thisismars    17 min ago
ya my best friends are missing

galaxygenius    16 min ago
maybe OP can help

# 4
# LIGHTS, CAMERA, DETENTION

**T**oothpick was usually the first one to get to detention because he had his backpack all ready to go in sixth period. While everyone else was still packing up at their lockers, he made his way down the sixth-grade hall, past the mural of rocket ships, which was cool even though everyone knows the fins on the rockets are supposed to point down, not out. When Toothpick had tried to tell Principal Fagan, she'd made that pressed line with her lips as if she were going to vomit.

A lot of teachers got that look when Toothpick tried to explain something they were doing wrong. He never understood why people who were supposedly interested in teaching didn't want to get it right themselves. Toothpick's mom explained that some people were sensitive to suggestions. "Better to keep quiet, Randall" is what she said.

He tried, but it was hard.

He continued through the seventh-grade hall that had the mural with the aliens (who oddly resembled the lunch staff), and then it was down the metal staircase to detention, where Mr. Q had already arrived. Toothpick always sat in the same desk near the front, closest to the door. This way he could see who was coming. Mostly it was his friends, but occasionally there would be other people like Clyde Boofsky and his pals, in which case it made sense to sit as far from the back as possible to avoid getting paper objects (dry or wet) thrown at his head.

Toothpick was arranging his homework assignments on his desk when he saw Mars.

"Why am I always here?" Mars said, his headphones still hanging around his neck. "Like, I don't even remember when I *didn't* have detention."

"Me too," Toothpick said agreeably. "But at least I get to finish my homework."

Caddie came in next and sat down behind Mars. Her backpack landed on the ground with a thud. "Hey Mars, did you find Jonas? You both weren't at lunch."

Mars shook his head. "I had to take a math test." He held up a baseball cap. "But look what I found."

"That's Jonas's!" Caddie exclaimed.

Toothpick pushed his glasses up. "Jonas without his baseball cap? Highly atypical."

Toothpick knew because he'd been with Jonas when he

bought it at a Mariners game. Jonas had had it on when he'd caught a foul ball, and he'd worn his cap every day from then on.

"Because he was wearing it when he caught that fly ball," Mars said.

"Foul ball," Toothpick corrected.

"Geez, Pick," Mars said good-naturedly. "Same difference."

"Jonas wears his Mariners cap," Toothpick said, "because he thinks it will bring him good luck when taking tests and talking to girls."

"Wait, what?" Caddie asked, smiling.

"That's why Jonas wouldn't just leave it in the boys' bathroom," Mars said. "So where is he? I've texted him— no answer. I called his home phone—the number is no longer in service. It's just like Aurora!"

"You're right," Toothpick said. "That's two unexplainable disappearances."

It wasn't the first time Aurora had been absent, so Toothpick hadn't thought much of it. In fact, he never talked to her except in detention. She was the only other person he knew who watched his favorite show, *Ancient Aliens*. She had her own theories about alien life. *Aliens didn't just build the pyramids, Pick,* she said to him. *They're the ones inside it. Why else are the mummies wrapped up?* Toothpick didn't have a good answer. Most of the time though, Aurora was on her phone, texting Mars.

Aurora being gone—not strange. But Jonas?

"Do you think Jonas moved away?" Caddie asked.

"In the middle of the school day?" Mars asked.

"Folks, let's get this show on the road," said Mr. Q, who had whipped out his neon-green clipboard. He was very particular about attendance. Other than that, though, he wasn't too bad. Sometimes he brought treats to detention, but they were usually the healthy kind with flaxseed and raisins. Mostly he read the newspaper, and kids could do whatever they wanted as long as they were quiet and didn't use their phones.

"I'd hardly call this a show," Mars said glumly.

"Life is a show," Mr. Q said, taking out his pen. "Don't you kids know that? We're all being watched. *We're all stars in the making.*"

Mars looked up suddenly. "What did you say?"

"I said," Mr. Q said, enunciating each word carefully, "life is a show, Mars. Ah, Epica, can I help you?"

Epica Hernandez had sailed into the room with a sheet of paper in her hand. She was wearing a dark gray turtleneck, pleated miniskirt, and laced up combat boots. Her fingernails were painted red today. "There were a few updates to the attendance," she announced breezily, handing the sheet to Mr. Q. "Like, more hours added for some people." When she said that, she stared straight at Mars.

"Way to be obvious," Mars said. "Or maybe you're talking about all *your* hours."

Epica tossed her hair back. "I've never been in detention. Not unless you count the extra credit I get for helping out in the main office after school. But that's a job reserved for honors students. You're probably not familiar with that."

"Yeah, well, you keep reminding us," Mars said.

"That will be all, Epica," Mr. Q said. "Thank you for the updated sheet."

"You're welcome," she said. On her way out, she looked at Toothpick. "Hi, Randall."

For some reason, Epica always made a point of saying hi to Toothpick. And there was something Toothpick hadn't told anyone—he kind of liked it.

"Uh, hi," he said back. "You can call me Toothpick if you want."

She smiled. "I like Randall better."

Toothpick's neck turned red. "Um, yeah," he mumbled, and quickly looked at his homework.

After Epica left, Mr. Q attached the new attendance sheet to his clipboard. "Caddie Patchett?" he called out.

"Here," she said. "But, uh, you can see that."

Mr. Q said, "We're making this official. Caddie Patchett, check. Here for unruly behavior."

"It was an accident. The books fell out of the cart," Caddie said.

"Yeah, I was her reading partner yesterday, and I knocked them out," Mars said.

"JP McGowan?" Mr. Q called out. "Is she here?"

"Are they here, you mean," Toothpick said. "That's the pronoun JP uses."

Mr. Q said, "Sorry. You're right. Are they here? Looks like no. Randall Lee?"

"Here," Toothpick said. "But as I keep saying, no one calls me that. Unless you're my mom."

"Or Epica," Mars said, grinning, which made Toothpick's neck turn red again.

"Check," Mr. Q said. "Here for correcting the math teacher too many times and causing a disruption."

"The teacher was solving for $x$ when he should have been solving for $y$," Toothpick explained. "I was pointing it out."

"Yeesh," Mars said. "This school has the dumbest reasons for detention."

"Mars Patel, check," Mr. Q went on. "Here for insubordination, answering back to authority, and being a general pain in the—"

Mr. Q was interrupted by a figure squeezing past him and sliding into a chair.

"Hi, y'all. What did I miss?" JP asked breathlessly. "Sorry I'm late."

"JP McGowan, at last," Mr. Q said, eyeing them. "Here for destruction of school property."

"That's a new one," Toothpick said. "Well, not really."

"I closed the window in Spanish and the glass broke," JP said proudly. "Seriously, y'all, I don't know my own strength."

Mr. Q was reading through the list. "Aurora Gershowitz? Still not here. And what about Jonas Hopkins?"

"They're both missing," Mars said despondently.

"Wait, Jonas, too? I thought it was just Aurora," JP said.

"Jonas disappeared during the Code Red," Caddie explained.

"OK, detention has officially started. No talking and no cell phones. Please take out your homework and save your discussion for later," Mr. Q told everyone.

Mars tapped his fingers impatiently against the desk. Usually he didn't do any of his homework in detention. Usually he was devising the next plan for disrupting life at H. G. Wells. Two weeks ago during recess, he and Aurora had switched all the lights in their English teacher's room with bulbs they could control remotely with their phones. All during class, Mars would turn the lights on and off, even changing the colors to neon yellow and green, until

Ms. DeTemple was ready to have a nervous breakdown. Then last week, they got ahold of Clyde Boofsky's phone and replaced the ringtone with a giant farting sound. They kept calling him so he sounded like he was ripping big ones in front of everyone in science. The Boof yelled at everyone to stop laughing, then he was sent to the nurse's office for "excessive flatulence."

But today? Zilch. No ideas. With Aurora and Jonas gone, what was the point? Shouldn't he be thinking about how to get them back?

Behind Mars, JP was sketching out a game plan for the upcoming soccer match. Today their team was leaving the school at four thirty for an away game. "Hey Mr. Q, OK if I leave a few minutes early?" JP called out. "My bus leaves for Bremerton in thirty minutes."

Mr. Q glanced over his newspaper. "We've gone over this before. I have a note from your coach. They'll wait if you leave here immediately after detention. That gives you three minutes to get to the bus out front."

"Only if I run," JP muttered. JP could do most things if they required being strong or fast. It was waiting that sucked.

"What happened to Jonas?" JP whispered to Mars.

"I don't know," he whispered back. "I think it has something to do with Aurora."

"There is a high probability," Toothpick agreed, looking

up from his science homework, which he'd already finished so he was making up a few extra problems for his
teacher to solve. "Of course, there's a low probability, too.
Depends on the variables."

"Like what?" Caddie whispered.

Toothpick listed them. "Time of day, clues found, moti-
vations, hostile presences, weather patterns."

"That's everything, Pick," JP scoffed.

"Ow," Caddie suddenly said, pressing her head.

Toothpick jerked a thumb in her direction. "Oh, yeah,
and Caddie's head."

The newspaper rustled violently. "I can hear everything," Mr. Q called out. "You really don't know what quiet
means, do you?"

Mars cleared his throat. "Maybe we're not who you want
us to be."

Mr. Q put down his paper, which was open to an article
titled "No Time for Plan B—Climate Change Is Happening
Now." "What does that mean, Mars?" he asked.

JP let out a big sigh. "Look, everybody in this school
hates us because of who we are."

"Who are we?" Caddie asked, surprised.

"Freaks," JP answered. "Outcasts, misfits."

"Losers," Toothpick added.

"Hey," Caddie said indignantly.

"I know what you're saying, JP," Mr. Q said. "You're

right that the school doesn't view your gang favorably. In fact, the principal has some choice words for all of you. You wouldn't be able to get into Pruitt Prep with *her* recommendation."

"Great," Mars muttered. "So we're delinquents."

Mr. Q's face softened. "Look, you're not here because you're bad kids. You're here because you're smart kids but you haven't figured out how to stay out of trouble."

"Really?" JP asked. "You think we're smart?"

Mr. Q smiled. "I'm not the only one who thinks so. But it's like that time you reprogrammed the sprinkler system to go off during track practice? That was awful. Brilliant, but awful."

Mars grinned. That was a sick prank. And now Mr. Q calling it brilliant? Hearing that got the juices in Mars's brain flowing again.

"Plus, I see how you treat each other," Mr. Q said, "and the things you wonder about, and I think you kids are all right."

"Thanks, Mr. Q," JP said. "You're all right, too."

Mr. Q picked up the newspaper again. "But just because I think that doesn't mean you get to talk in detention. Rules are rules. Remember, they have cameras in every room. Somebody's watching you right now."

This made everyone automatically look up at the two tiny lenses in the far corners of the ceiling. Mr. Q was talking about the new security system that had been installed over the summer.

Meanwhile, Mars had sat back in his chair. "All right, Mr. Q, we'll be quiet," he said casually.

Toothpick, Caddie, and JP immediately looked at him. Something was up. They could hear the change in Mars's voice.

He leaned over to them. "I have a plan to find Jonas," he whispered. "Who's free after nine tonight?"

"Ooooh, count me in!" JP whispered right away.

"Affirmative," Toothpick whispered.

"Nine o'clock?" Caddie repeated. "That's, like, after dark. My parents will be home."

"What's it going to be, Cads?" Mars said. "To the stars!"

Caddie swallowed. "I guess I could climb out my window." She glanced at Mr. Q, whose eyes were glued to his newspaper. "But Mars, what on earth are you getting us into?"

# 5

# A PROMISE
# IS A PROMISE

The first time Aurora had talked to Mars was on the first day of sixth grade, when she'd told him he was sitting in her seat.

"Move," she said. "That's my chair. I saw the seating chart."

Mars looked at her, slightly terrified. Were they supposed to have assigned seats already in English? It didn't matter. Mars got up readily and moved his things off the desk because Aurora Gershowitz was scary. Not scary like Clyde Boofsky or Scott Bane, who were big and tough but total dumb-heads. Aurora was scary because she was pretty. She'd been in his fourth- and fifth-grade classes, and everything she did seemed to be an act of defiance, from her purple-tipped hair to her spiky wristbands to her bright red lipstick when no other girls were wearing makeup. She was also really smart, which meant she would finish her work way before everyone else did and wander off into the hall until someone brought her back and said they'd found her opening a locked door, gluing shut an open one, turning lights on and off, and generally being a nuisance.

As Mars stood there with his notebook and pencil, Aurora seemed to reconsider.

"Actually, your chair is in front of me," she said. "So you better sit there."

Sit in front of Aurora Gershowitz? Wasn't that *more* terrifying? Mars sat down anyway, conscious of all the awful things Aurora could do to him with his back turned: make faces, shoot rubber bands, laugh at him. But then something unexpected happened. A piece of folder paper landed in his lap. It was a note from Aurora. For the next few incredible minutes, the piece of paper went back and forth between them as Ms. DeTemple was busy loading a program on the SMART Board.

*Why is your name Mars?*

NICKNAME

*cool nickname*

And then:

*Want to rearrange DeTemple's desk when she isn't looking?*

WHAT DO YOU MEAN? WHY?

*To mess with her*

When Ms. DeTemple announced she was getting something from the office and would be back shortly, Mars turned around and saw Aurora grinning at him. It was a smile Mars would come to recognize again and again, whenever Aurora was up to no good.

They scrambled to the front desk: pencil case moved to the right, papers to the left, books piled on the chair. The rest of the class watched with mild interest. It didn't occur to anyone to stop them. Then as a last thought, Mars lay the computer monitor facedown.

When Ms. DeTemple came back and Aurora and Mars were back in their seats, she stopped and looked at her desk, wondering what had happened. The worst was when she tried to get the SMART Board to work and the computer screen flashed some strange, blinking images of a gorilla. Then Ms. DeTemple became really alarmed. Did she have a computer virus? Or was she just going crazy? It was a stupid prank, but that moment when the rest of the class giggled and poked one another was *huge*.

That's when Mars got it. This was what Aurora did. She caused disruption. *Live a little, Mars*, she told him. *Piss people off*. She never explained why. But that wasn't the point. Being with Aurora was what mattered. And if he could help her, he could talk to her, too.

So he came up with the ideas, and Aurora gleefully helped carry them out: sliming toilet seats, locking computer screens with photoshopped images of Fagan wearing antlers on her head, taping beeping circuit boards under the desks in the main office, turning off the main water supply at school. Each new prank gave Aurora fresh delight. And made her like Mars more. Of course, they always got caught. Which meant detention, which meant more time with Aurora. Which was fine with Mars.

The only person not fine with it was his mom.

"Why all these detentions now?" she exclaimed. "Mars, what is happening to you?"

He wasn't sure. Except that he was having the time of his life. And his friends were, too.

At first, JP, Caddie, Jonas, and Toothpick had been skeptical. Why waste your time pranking the school when it just meant landing in detention? And who was this Aurora anyway? None of them had talked to her before. Then one by one, Mars started enlisting their help—Jonas and Caddie played lookout while Mars and Aurora switched the light bulbs. JP distracted the Boof by enraging him with "Boof jokes" ("What do you get when you cross the Boof with a math test? A zero!") while Mars grabbed his phone in math. And Toothpick? Toothpick simply loved the challenge of not getting caught. Even though most of the time they did, thanks to those pesky security cameras.

Still, pulling off pranks—it was the most fun they'd ever had. Plus, detention meant they could hang out and chill together, and middle school was bearable.

Then last week Aurora had been really upset. In English, she didn't say a word. In the lunchroom on Tuesday, Aurora said she wanted to be alone, and she sat by herself, drawing in her sketchbook. After school, she skipped detention.

That day, right after Mr. Q read off the attendance sheet in detention, Mars got a text from Aurora.

## Mars · Aurora

Tues, Oct 13, 3:11 pm

Aurora
**meet me back door nr graffiti**

Mars
**wut abt detention**

Aurora
**skip**

Mars
**b there in 2**


    Mars got up to use the bathroom. He'd never skipped detention before, so he figured Mr. Q wouldn't suspect anything. He walked quietly down the hall to the back door of the school, conscious of the security cameras along the way. Would one of them see him leaving detention? Would Mr. Q get notified? Maybe if Mars hurried, no one would notice right away.

    The back door locked from the inside, so Mars used a rock to prop it open. Aurora was waiting for him. She looked like a mess. Her mascara was running, and her hair was wet. It must have just rained. It was always raining in Port Elizabeth.

    "Aurora—are you OK?" he asked immediately.

    "He was supposed to come," she said, her voice ragged. "First he said he'd come this morning. Then he said lunch. Then he said he'd come in the afternoon. I waited here an hour. Now I get a text from him, and he's calling it off."

    "Who?" Mars said.

    "My dad," Aurora said. "We were driving to Port Townsend. He was supposed to be here."

    "I thought you weren't talking to him," Mars said

cautiously. Aurora's dad had left when she was little, and now lived about an hour away, near Tacoma. But she rarely saw him. The last time was a few years ago, and it had ended badly, with her parents yelling at each other and him driving away fast in his car.

Mars had told her about his dad leaving, too, when he was three. It was something they shared—the emptiness of their dads not being around.

"Maybe something came up," Mars said. "Maybe he'll send another text."

"Yeah, well, up his," Aurora said. She wiped her nose with the back of her hand. "I don't need him. I don't need people who promise things and then don't do what they promise. A promise is a promise."

"A promise is a promise," Mars agreed. He didn't know what else to say, so he gave her a hug. As she hugged him back, he could hear her heart beating loudly.

"You wouldn't do that, would you?" Aurora's voice was muffled. "Promise something and then not do it?"

"No," Mars said. "A promise is a promise."

"Yeah, I know that about you, Mars," she said softly. "You'd come if I needed you. Right?"

"Promise," Mars said.

Just then the back door opened, and the rock bounced away into a puddle.

"Aurora Gershowitz, Mars Patel." It was Principal Fagan, her voice like gravel. "Please report to detention right away. And this *will* double your hours, by the way."

Aurora stuck her tongue out at Fagan as they went back inside, following the principal down the hall. But she wasn't crying anymore, her arm looped inside Mars's so they were walking together, their shoes hitting the floor in unison.

Mars breathed in and out. They were friends, but they were more than friends. He'd always come through for her, and now she knew. *A promise is a promise.*

That was the last time he'd seen Aurora.

15 ▶ 30 ∿∿∿

One caller asks:

"Oliver, how did you get to be so successful?"

Well, I might have private jets and rocket ships
(yes, plural!),
but that's not what makes me successful.
It's because I BUILD BRAINS FOR THE FUTURE.

Here's a riddle:
I am weightless, yet you can see me.
Put me in a basket, and I'll make it lighter.
What am I?
First kid to call in the answer wins a prize!
But you're all winners, right?

To the stars!

410 Comments

allie_j   44 min ago
I know but I'm not saying

galaxygenius   20 min ago
it's gonna be on the gift test right

wanna_b   18 min ago
my dad says OP is fake

staryoda   15 min ago
maybe your dad is fake

thisismars   10 min ago
OP is the real deal

# 6
# NOBODY HOME

**T**he plan was pretty simple. They would meet in front of Jonas's house at nine and knock on the front door. If no one answered, they would break in to look for clues. Mars had never done something like that before. But what could go wrong?

At home, dinner consisted of Galaxy Clusters—clusters of oats, nuts, and chocolatey goodness floating in a bowl of cold milk. It was Mars's standard meal when his mom wasn't home, and lately that was often. Why she was even working two jobs in the first place, he didn't know. Couldn't his dad help out, too, wherever he was? Sometimes his mom prayed in the puja room off the kitchen, and he could hear her reciting words in Sanskrit while lighting a stick of incense. And then it was work, work, work. *Beta, it's all for you,* she would say. *I'll keep you safe.*

Safe from what? Mars wasn't even sure what she did. In

the mornings, she went somewhere with a loading dock, and she was in charge of what came off the boat from Puget Sound. Fish? Medical supplies? Then in the evening, she went someplace else where she had to change first into dark sweats. Mars asked her once if she was going to the gym. She just laughed and said she was filing papers. Who filed papers late into the night?

The front door opened and Saira Patel came bustling in.

"Mars, beta, no time to eat. How are you?" She stopped when she saw what Mars was eating. "Galaxy Clusters? Again? What did I tell you? Time to eat healthy. Did you see what I left for you in the fridge? Dal and rotis and . . ." She opened the refrigerator and looked in. "Oh. I thought I left it. I must have finished it already. Manu, I'm so sorry!"

"It's OK, Ma," Mars said.

She tousled his hair. "I had a scare today with that Code Red. Glad it was nothing. Maybe some kids pulling a prank? It wasn't you, was it, Mars? You're still a good child, beta. Even if you need a haircut. You're just like—" Her voice broke off.

"Just like who?" Mars asked even though he knew who and that Ma wouldn't talk about it. Instead, she looked at the clock. "Look at the time! I'm late! Must change and run, Mars!"

"Late for what?" Mars mumbled, but his mom had already disappeared inside her room. A few minutes later she came out wearing a dark turtleneck and black leggings. For a moment Mars pictured her scaling the Space Needle in Seattle or jumping into a dark hole, searching for buried treasure. Who knew?

Then suddenly he broke into a smile. "It's a hole, Ma. That's what makes a basket lighter."

"You have some funny ideas for baskets," she said, distracted. Before Mars could explain about the riddle from the podcast, she was already walking out the door. "Mars, I'll be back late, sweetie. I'll see you in you in the stars!"

"See you in the stars," Mars repeated, muttering. He doubted she had even heard him. They had been saying that to each other ever since he was little and she'd dropped him off at preschool for the first time. Back then she had told him not to worry, that she could see him wherever he was, even when she was far away. *We are in the stars, you and me,* she'd told him. *Always together.*

Well, was she with him right now?

Mars scooped up another spoonful of cereal and leafed through a brochure for Pruitt Prep. He'd gone through it so many times, the corners were dog-eared. The brochure had come in the mail a few months before, and he didn't know how they'd gotten his name or address—he hadn't even taken the GIFT test yet. The brochure was full of pictures of what students did there. Like build robots and cars and create special foods to make you smarter. One girl had invented an artificial plant that didn't need anything but sunlight, and two guys came up with infinite Ping-Pong— Mars wasn't even sure what that was, but they might still be playing it now. Infinite loops, artificial intelligence, speed. This was the stuff of Pruitt Prep.

Mars looked back at the envelope from Pruitt Prep. At least he assumed it was from them. The envelope had no return address, just his real name on it, the one he never used:

★ **Manu Patel, a Star in the Making** ★

A star in the making. That was what Mr. Q had said in detention today. Was it just a coincidence?

Mars finished his cereal and studied the pages with pictures of the front of the school. Seeing them now, something puzzled him. In one picture, the front of the school was covered with tall trees. But when Mars turned the page, the next photograph of the front showed a clear sky with no trees in sight. And there was a moon! How could the same building have two very different views from the front? Mars picked up his phone.

| Mars · Toothpick |
| :---: |

Mon, Oct 19, 8:32 pm

Mars
**can u edit trees out of a photo**

Toothpick
**Affirmative aka wonders of digital editing**

Mars
**Because buildings don't move**

Toothpick
**Affirmative**

Mars
**cool see u soon**

Toothpick
**Over and out**

🎧

**The sky was dark by the time Mars reached Jonas's house.**
They had agreed to meet across the street next to a large
pine tree.

"Hi, Mars," Toothpick said, his voice muffled.

Mars blinked. "What are you wearing, Pick?"

Toothpick had a dark ski mask covering his face so
that only his eyes and nose showed. "I bought this when
I was learning to ski on Bear Mountain. I thought I'd use
it now."

"I already told him he looks ridiculous," JP said. "This
isn't ski school."

Toothpick glanced at JP's soccer uniform and cleats.
"This isn't a soccer match, if we're getting technical."

"That's different. I didn't have time to change after I got
back," JP said. "We beat Bremerton 2–0. Thanks for asking." JP pulled out a sandwich. "And I'm still eating dinner."

"Where's Caddie?" Mars asked. "Is she still coming?"

"I'm here. I'm here." Caddie came up to them with a slight limp and a hole in the knee of her jeans.

"Whoa, what happened, Cads?" JP asked.

Caddie held out a hand. "I'd rather not say. It's too embarrassing. Let's just say a certain rosebush under my window and I aren't friends anymore."

"All right, guys," Mars said. "Everyone's here. Next step, one of us rings the doorbell, so we don't all call attention to ourselves."

"I'll do it," Toothpick volunteered. "And if no one's home?"

"We break in . . ." Mars whispered. He paused.

"Scared, Mars?" JP asked. "'Cause I'm ready to bust in there and get the job done."

Mars smiled. "OK, JP. But let's try not to break anything yet, huh?"

The gang watched Toothpick cross the street to Jonas's house. He walked silently and confidently, as if he'd done break-ins all his life.

"That's Toothpick: always chill," Mars said.

"Except for that stupid thing on his face. I'm sorry, but if I saw somebody walking by at night in a ski mask, I'd call the police." JP licked their fingers, finishing the last of a grilled chicken sandwich.

Caddie looked at Mars. "Did your mom ask you where you were going?"

He shrugged. "She's not even home. Like always."

"My parents are cool," JP said.

"They're OK with you here?" Caddie asked, surprised.

"Oh, I don't tell them stuff," JP said, grinning. "They think I'm asleep in bed."

"My parents would kill me if they saw me here," Caddie said. "They think I'm studying for the GIFT in my room."

By now, Toothpick was back. "No sign of Jonas or his family. I tried ringing the doorbell, then I scaled the perimeter."

"Say what?" JP asked.

"Good job, Pick. That leaves us with plan B." Mars's voice dropped low. "Look for rocks."

"I was worried about this," Caddie said.

Toothpick watched as everyone searched the ground. JP looked for the biggest rock. As they approached the house, each with a rock in hand, Toothpick finally spoke. "I guess your plan was to use the rocks to break a window?"

"Shush!" Mars whispered.

Toothpick pulled up his ski mask. "Wow, it's hard to breathe with this on. Anyway, the rocks aren't necessary and might call attention to us."

"What other choice do we have?" Mars whispered, his breath exploding in a sigh. "If we don't go inside now, maybe the only clues there to help us find Jonas will disappear. This is our best option right now."

"Affirmative," Toothpick said. "I just meant we didn't need the rocks. I know the code to disengage the alarm and open the door."

For a moment they stared at him.

Then JP started laughing. "That's my friend!"

Mars let his rock fall to the ground. "Come on, then. Let's go."

After Toothpick punched in the code, he opened the door and they all went in.

"I don't believe it!" Caddie said. "Where's the furniture?"

The home was stripped clean.

"He was just in school," she said. "How could his family move out so suddenly?"

Toothpick pulled off his ski mask. "Plus, Jonas didn't say anything."

Mars was opening a closet and looking inside. "Yeah, well, maybe he didn't know." He went to the staircase. "I'm checking Jonas's room."

"I'll come with you, Mars," JP offered right away.

"Pick and I will finish the first floor," Caddie said.

The lights were out upstairs, so they had to use the streetlights coming through the windows to see. They opened the closets in every room and looked behind the doors.

"How can anyone disappear in a day?" Mars wondered.

"They had help, Mars," JP said. "When my uncle got a

new job in Portland, his company moved him in a day. The moving company packed up everything, and boom, they were done."

By now they'd reached Jonas's room. Mars went to look out the window. Not because he expected Jonas to be standing outside on the street but because Mars needed a minute. This whole disappearing thing was getting under his skin.

The rain had lifted, but the sky was still overcast. Your typical October evening in Port Elizabeth. But Mars wasn't checking the weather. He was looking at the outline of the horizon, where the Puget Sound met the sky in the distance. Sometimes he thought if he looked long enough he would see something out of the ordinary—something more than just boats. It was silly. But when people went missing in your life, you found yourself looking for them in the strangest places. Like maybe they were there in the shadows of your life all along, but you weren't looking where you should be.

Now JP had found something in Jonas's closet. "Hey Mars, take a look at this."

It was a torn manila envelope.

"Let me hold it up to the window," Mars said. But before he could get a look, they both heard it: *ding*. A text notification. Mars reached for his phone, where a text flashed on the screen.

Mon, Oct 19, 9:42 pm

Aurora

**ad astra**

Mars's eyes bugged out. "It's from Aurora!"

JP was looking at their phone, too. "Ditto."

Caddie and Toothpick came clamoring up the stairs and into the room.

"We got a text from Aurora!" Toothpick called out.

"We all did, Pick," JP said.

*"Ad astra,"* Caddie said. "What does that mean?"

"It's Latin," JP said. "*Ad* means 'to.' Not sure about *astra.*"

"How do you know Latin?" Toothpick asked.

"I don't," JP said. "But my dad is a classics professor. You pick things up, you know."

Just then they heard them coming down the street: sirens. They all looked at one another.

"You don't think . . ." Caddie wondered.

The sirens got louder.

All this time Mars had been quiet. He was looking at the manila envelope in his hand, where the streetlight hit it. It was postmarked two days ago.

★ **Jonas Hopkins, a Star in the Making** ★

"Quick, somebody look up *ad astra,*" he said.

55

"On it," Toothpick said.

Meanwhile, the siren had stopped in front of Jonas's house. It was a police car, its flashing lights turning everyone's faces blue and red. There was a voice over a loudspeaker. "This is the police. Please exit the house at once. We know you're in there. We can see you."

"Guys . . ." Caddie moaned.

"There's no way out, guys," JP said. "Pick, I thought you disengaged the alarm!"

"I think I just unlocked the front door," Toothpick said ruefully. "Now I remember—Jonas said if the alarm isn't fully turned off, it silently calls the police. No warning."

Downstairs, they could hear the front door banging open.

"Great! Caught!" JP groaned. "Mars, you haven't said a word."

"Pick, what does *ad astra* mean?" Mars yelled.

"We're caught, Mars! No time left!" JP yelled back.

The sound of people entering echoed through the house. "Come out now. This is the police!" Then footsteps on the stairs.

"Hurry, Pick," Mars urged.

Toothpick's phone had found the answer. "It means 'to the stars,'" he called out.

Caddie gasps. "Wait, that's . . ."

And then it was like Armageddon as the police stormed the room.

# POLICE DEPARTMENT OF PORT ELIZABETH

## JUVENILE INCIDENT REPORT

NAME
Manu Patel

HAIR COLOR
black

EYE COLOR
black

AGE
11

ADDRESS
343 Chinook St., Apt. 3, Port Elizabeth, WA

DATE OF INCIDENT
October 19

TIME OF REPORTING
11:30 p.m.

NAMES OF OTHERS APPREHENDED
Caddie Patchett, Juniper P. McGowan, Randall Lee

REPORTED INCIDENT
Patel and cohorts caught breaking and entering at 8 Douglas
Fir Circle, previously belonging to owners Rutherford and
Mary Hopkins, who had since vacated. No items reported
broken or missing YET. Patel claimed to be looking for missing
friend, Jonas, when it appeared the entire family had moved
out officially two days prior. According to records, Patel has
a long record of infractions and disruptions at H. G. Wells
Middle School, where he is a sixth grader. Patel detained at
department until mother, Saira Patel, arrived and assumed
responsibility at 11:00 p.m., after night shift ended. No
charges pressed against Manu Patel for now, but issued a
warning. His school has been notified.

REPORTING OFFICER
Samuel Kaiser

## Mars · Caddie · JP · Toothpick

Tues, Oct 20, 12:20 am

Mars
guys sry

Caddie
did u just get home Mars?!

Mars
police had so many Qs

JP
anyone else grounded

Mars
meee

Caddie
my parents still deciding

they were too mad at the police station

Toothpick
no science channel for a month

JP
aw sry Pick

Mars
anyone hear from Aurora again

JP
gawd mars think about someone else for a change

Mars
but she said ad astra!!!

**JP**
it means to the stars so what

**Toothpick**
I think mars is talking about the podcast

**Mars**
OP says it every time

**JP**
Again so what

**Caddie**
sry guys falling asleep GN

**Mars**
GN caddie

**JP**
Gn

**Toothpick**
over and out

---

**Mars · Aurora**

Tues, Oct 20, 12:30 am

**Mars**
Aurora?

**Mars**
we got ur msg did u mean who I think u mean??

Tues, Oct 20, 12:48 am

**Mars**
weird the cops came right after you texted

Tues, Oct 20, 12:56 am

Mars

**r u even getting these**

Tues, Oct 20, 12:58 am

Mars

**sry I keep texting it helps me think**

Tues, Oct 20, 1:02 am

Mars

**the envelope for jonas is another clue right**

15 ▶ 30

Podcast listeners,
do you know what it means to hit a snag?
Here's a secret.
Maybe you think your parents are going to work.
Ever wonder if it's true?
If they're building that bridge, designing that tunnel,
WORKING THAT SECOND SHIFT?
What if it's your parent who's hit the snag?

To the stars!

432 Comments ⌃

godzilla    20 min ago
my dad goes to the arcade when he says he's working #snag

allie_j    18 min ago
my mom flunked the bar exam twice #snag

neptunebaby    15 min ago
my brother can't tie his shoelaces & he's 16!! #snag

wormhole    12 min ago
my cousin in australia says kids are missing #missingkids

godzilla    10 min ago
omg here in texas too. Does anyone know why #missingkids

galaxygenius    18 min ago
OP have you hit a snag

lostinlondon    5 min ago
Sometimes a snag means ur rly close

# WAIT, WHAT?

**M**ars was in bed, lights off, the podcast running in his ears, when he suddenly sat up. Had he heard right? Mars hit rewind.

*Ever wonder if that's true?*
*If they're building that bridge, designing that tunnel,*
*WORKING THAT SECOND SHIFT?*

Wait a minute. *What?*

Because Mars did wonder about his mom's second shift. He did wonder why she didn't have a normal job. JP's dad was a professor, and their mom was a lawyer. Caddie's parents were teachers. Toothpick's dad was a dentist, and his mom worked in a bank. Normal jobs with normal hours. Mars didn't even know what his mom did.

What if she was involved in something dangerous? What if it was shady or against the law? When Mars and his mother had driven to Tacoma last weekend, there had been picketers on both sides of the highway. On one side there were signs that read: HUMAN RIGHTS 4 ALL HUMANS. On the other side: ILLEGALS, GO HOME. He'd asked his mom, *Are we illegal?* She said, *No, of course not.* She had shown him his papers before. Even so, Mars was never sure.

Mars listened to the podcast over and over. It made no sense. And yet in some mysterious way, it did. Didn't the podcast say before that something big was going to happen? Then something had. Aurora and Jonas were *both* gone. And now it said his mom was lying to him. Just where did Ma go on her second shift? Did Oliver know something Mars didn't? Was Oliver trying to warn him?

**From:** dfagan@hgwellsmiddeschool.org
**To:** Saira Patel <eyesontheprize@zapmail.com>
**Date:** Tuesday, October 20, 6:30 a.m.
**Subject:** Urgent: Immediate Action Requested

Dear Ms. Patel,

It has come to our attention that Manu Patel was apprehended by the Port Elizabeth Police last night for breaking and entering. We find your son's behavior deeply troubling. As you know, our school's motto is "Every Success for Every Child." And by success, we don't mean incarceration. Please report to the school office with Manu this morning at 8:00 a.m. SHARP so we can discuss his academic future.

Sincerely,
Dorena Fagan
Principal
H. G. Wells Middle School

From: Saira Patel <eyesontheprize@zapmail.com>
To: dfagan@hgwellsmiddeschool.org
Date: Tuesday, October 20, 6:37 a.m.
Subject: We will be there!!!

Dear Principal Fagan,

Mars is so, so sorry!! He will not do it again—breaking in or entering anyone's houses. He is grounded, meaning he stays at home doing his homework—THAT'S IT. You can have my word. We are both sincerely sorry. We will meet with you to discuss Mars's future. Perhaps he needs new friends. And more homework. Can you tell me again when the GIFT test is?

Sincerely,
Saira Patel

**In the car on the way to school, Ma went over everything:** Don't mention last night. Don't mention the police. Don't mention Officer Kaiser.

"Ma, the school knows what happened," Mars said, exasperated. "That's why we're going."

"Well, you don't have to *talk* about it," she said. "Sometimes they're trying to get you to say things so they can punish you more."

"What can they do now anyway? Give me detention for life?"

They watched as a school bus turned in front of them. Then Ma continued, telling Mars all the reasons he had to shape up, that detention was no place for him. At the stoplight her eyes fell on him.

"What, looking at your phone again?" she asked, irritated. "Did you even hear one word I said? Always listening to that podcast! That Oliver Pruitt, he can't—" She bit her lip.

"He can't what?" Mars asked pointedly. "At least he tries to be helpful. He isn't lying about himself like . . ."

Ma gave him an incredulous look as if he'd told her the world was spun out of cotton candy.

"Oliver Pruitt tries to be *helpful*?" she repeated. "Well, that's a first!" Her eyes narrowed. "What did you mean about the other part? About him not lying? Is someone else lying to you?"

"It doesn't matter," Mars mumbled. "And I wasn't listening to the podcast. I was reading the comments. Did you know a bunch of kids are missing around the world? And no one knows why."

The light turned green. "Missing kids, huh?" Saira asked, her eyes back on the road.

"It's wrong, Ma. Whether it's someone else or your best friends." Mars stared out the window. "I can't keep letting it happen."

Ma drove on for a moment, but instead of continuing into the school lot, she suddenly veered to the right and pulled up to the curb.

"Whoa. What's going on?" Mars asked, surprised.

She shut off the engine and looked at him very intently. "Mars. Mars, beta. I get what this is about. You can't be worrying about everybody else. You think if you find Aurora, it's like you finding your dad."

"No, don't start that," Mars groaned. "Why do you need to have theories about me? I'm fine."

"I'm serious. You carry that in you, and you shouldn't. Mars, you are very special. I have always known that about you." Her face softened. "You will do many wonderful things in your life."

"Then why do I keep screwing up?" Mars asked.

"Don't see it that way. Look at all the science contests

you have won. And that automated glove warmer. Very clever. I use it every day."

"Yeah, well, it ignited Mrs. Baker's desk in science. That's one of the reasons I'm in detention."

"You think so? And not because of the flashing light bulbs in English class, or the beeping circuit board in the principal's office?" Saira's voice was pointed. "Sometimes Mars, you are brilliant. And sometimes you are a buffoon. All these tricks you play on the school? Why? You need to *think* before you act, beta. Thinking is your strongest weapon." Her cell phone rang. She looked to see who it was. "I have to take this." She answered the phone. "Tell me," she said. *"Tumne kya suna hai?"* She continued in Hindi, talking in a low voice for about a minute. "OK, OK. *Theek hai.*" She hung up.

"Who was that?"

She started up the car and drove back into the street. "Nobody. My brother."

"Brother?" As far as Mars knew, his mom was an only child.

"OK, kind of a brother. Everybody is a brother when you're in India."

This was a weird explanation. Plus, now she seemed distracted, like there was something she wasn't telling him. Mars studied her face for clues, but her eyes were stony and unreadable. *Are you hitting a snag?* he wondered.

After they parked and walked inside the school to the main office, Ma reminded Mars about everything all over again. "Be your best," she pleaded with Mars as they stood outside the principal's door. "Listen to what Principal Fagan tells you. This might be your last chance, Mars."

∩

**Fagan didn't care to hear the other side of the story.**

"This is very concerning to our school's reputation," she said as soon as Mars and his mom sat down. "Every year, our students take the GIFT test, and every year, a handful of our very best gain admission to Pruitt Prep. That's not magic. We're lucky to get those precious few slots because we have a special relationship with Pruitt Prep. And while it takes years to build a solid reputation, it only takes a few minutes to destroy it." She looked hard at Mars.

"Surely what Mars did can't affect the rest of the school," Ma murmured nervously.

But Fagan was on a different mission. "It's not just Mars who was caught," she continued frostily. "We have already talked to Caddie's, Randall's, and JP's parents over the phone. They have all assured me that this kind of thing won't happen again. I believe them. Because Mars, even though your friends are a group of misguided misfits, there is still a chief instigator. And that person is you."

"I'm not an instigator," Mars said hotly. "What about Aurora and Jonas? Has anyone figured out where they've gone?"

"Aurora and Jonas are not your concern," Fagan said. "Let's focus on your disruptive tendencies and how we can stop them from affecting your friends. They have received a warning. And you, Mars, a one-day suspension from school. Starting now."

"Suspension!" Ma gasped. "That will look terrible on his transcript."

"It looks better than expulsion," Fagan said calmly. "We'll see you back in school tomorrow, Mr. Patel. With no more problems, I might add."

Outside the principal's office, Saira Patel finally glared at Mars. "Manu . . . what am I going to do with you? You heard what the principal said. Your disruptive behavior is affecting everyone—your friends, but most of all you. You can't be sneaking around at night."

"But Jonas and Aurora—"

"You can't be worried about them. Don't you see, Mars? It's time you stopped hanging around them. It's time you got serious."

"But they're my *friends*."

"No, I'm starting to see it now—what the problem is." Ma's voice wavered. "Maybe it was wrong to live in Port Elizabeth. There are too many distractions, too many problems. We shouldn't be here. We should go far, far away. We should live with my cousin in Cleveland."

She had thrown this line at Mars before, about her cousin in Cleveland. It was the last thing Mars wanted to hear.

Her phone rang again. She turned it on. "I said I will," she said tersely, and hung up. She saw Mars watching her. "I really have to go."

"Was that your 'brother,' again?"

Ma looked uncomfortable. "Listen, Mars, can you promise me you will go straight home? No talking to anyone, no hanging around. Go straight home and text me when you're there."

Mars wanted to find out more about who had called her, but just then behind her, he saw Caddie coming in through the front door.

"Fine, Ma," he said to her hurriedly. "I promise."

Saira looked at him uncertainly, and then she was gone, her shoes making a light tapping sound on the hallway floor.

Fagan poked her head out of her office. "Mars Patel? Are you still here? You do understand what a suspension is?"

Mars cringed, seeing students in the hallway turning to gawk at him. After Fagan went back into her office, he ran up to Caddie. "Cads, hey, wait up!" He hadn't seen her since they'd been separated at the police station the night before.

She stopped to give him a furtive look. "Mars—I'm not supposed to talk to you. My parents are really mad."

"But Caddie," Mars said slowly. "I didn't show you what JP found. I think I have an idea where to go, but I need your help."

"Mars, I can't." Caddie looked unhappy. "My parents are now saying they want to send me to boarding school in New Hampshire."

"New Hampshire?" Mars repeated. "But that's so far away. Why?"

"I don't know. They think *you're* a bad influence, Mars. They think you're the reason I'm always getting into trouble."

"I *am* the reason you're getting into trouble," Mars said. "But that's, like, our thing."

"Well, they think I'm going to screw up the GIFT, too," Caddie said. She pointed to a poster for Pruitt Prep on the wall where a life-size Oliver Pruitt watched them, smiling. "The test is in two days."

"You're going to do great, Caddie. How hard can the GIFT be?"

"I'm not like you, Mars," she said. "I need to study, not get distracted. And I *don't* want to go to New Hampshire."

Her eyes were dark pools of sadness behind her glasses. "I'm sorry, Mars. You're going to have to do whatever it is without me."

"But Cads," Mars said. "You're the one who balances me—"

"I don't think so, Mars." She cut him off. "Not anymore." She hurried away down the hall.

Mars stared at the Pruitt Prep poster. He'd thought the day couldn't get worse, but it just had. Aurora was gone. Jonas was gone. He was suspended. He was probably going to fail the GIFT. And now he had nothing left, not even Caddie to help him figure out where his life was going.

In front of him, Oliver Pruitt continued to smile mutely, as if he had all the answers but he just wouldn't say.

"How do I get to the stars?" Mars wondered out loud. He pulled his hood over his head and walked out into the misty morning.

## 8

# MIDDLE SCHOOL BLUES

**E**pica Hernandez had a big bow on her head today, and to JP, it seemed like the perfect target. Maybe a spitball would get Epica to shut up for once, JP thought. Just one quick lob and—

"I heard Mars Patel broke the law," Epica announced to anyone listening. "He's expelled. Which means he won't take the GIFT this week."

"Dude, Mars is expelled because no one can stand him," Clyde Boofsky said.

JP glared at them both. "He's suspended, not expelled, OK? He'll be here to take the GIFT, Epica. And I bet he'll do tons better than you."

Epica was unimpressed. "Maybe I should call him at home and ask if he needs help studying. And, like, charge him money for it. That's the only way Mars will pass the GIFT."

The spitball idea was looking more and more appealing. Too bad it wasn't JP's style—leave that to the Boof. On the other hand, Epica had brought up something else that was weighing on JP's mind. Mars at home, all alone.

JP looked up at the board where Mr. Green was going over algebra homework, and raised a hand. "Mr. Green? Can I go to the nurse's office? I think I'm going to barf."

Mr. Green turned around warily. "Are you sure?"

JP stood up in front of a sea of faces. Epica looked nervous and the Boof was snickering.

"I might hurl any moment, and I can't control where it lands," JP said, staring at Clyde Boofsky. "Like remember last week?" That got the Boof to stop laughing.

Last Monday JP'd coughed up a can of root beer all over Clyde's desk. Aurora had had an extra can of root beer that JP guzzled too quickly right before walking into algebra. It was great upchucking it all over the Boof's binder

Mr. Green relented at last. "Hurry," he said.

JP practically sprinted out the door. Their stomach was fine. It was Mars they were worried about. If they knew Mars, the one thing he hated was being by himself. Why else was he always getting himself into trouble? So he could be with the rest of them in detention. Duh.

JP didn't bother stopping at their locker. There was nothing they needed, just their phone, and the battery died anyway right as JP stepped outside the school. Gawd,

JP never remembered to charge it until it drained. Somebody needed to come up with an invention to help you remember all the things you needed to remember and forget all the things you didn't.

Because even if JP forgot to charge their battery, they never forgot the stupid things people said to them. Like Clyde Boofksy always did that thing where he pretend-sneezed and said "boy-girl" as soon as JP sat down.

But it wasn't just the Boof.

JP's mom could be hurtful, too. This morning she'd said, "Why don't you wear something different, honey? Wouldn't it be easier?"

JP grimaced. "My clothes are how I show the real me. Don't you get it?"

JP's mom didn't. Not really. Because every time she read in the newspaper about someone getting harassed, she got scared the same thing would happen to JP. Recently in Seattle, someone beat up a teenager wearing a skirt on a bus because they didn't look like a girl or a boy. The teenager ended up needing stitches.

"The world still sees everything gendered," JP's mom said. "We don't, but they do."

JP looked at their outfit: Arsenal sweatshirt, sparkly orange scarf, fleece shorts, multicolored leg warmers. Arsenal was JP's favorite soccer team, orange their favorite color, shorts were good for running, and leg warmers were cozy for when it rained, and it always rained in Port Elizabeth. It made sense to JP. The rest of the world needed to get on the same page.

When JP got to the apartment building, they climbed up the branch of a nearby tree. Climbing came naturally to JP. They liked to feel their muscles work as they pulled themself up. Mars's room was on the third floor—an easy jump from the tree to the fire escape outside Mars's window.

He was lying on his bed when JP rapped on his window.

"Open up, Mars! I don't have all day," JP called.

Mars jumped up in surprise. The window squeaked as he pushed it open. "What are you doing here, JP? Aren't you supposed to be . . . ?"

"Yeah, yeah, algebra," they said. "Who has time for that? Figured I'd bother you instead."

Mars's face brightened. "You didn't have to come," he said apologetically. "I don't want you in more trouble. What about your parents? Weren't they mad about the police?"

"Nah, don't worry. I can take care of myself." JP looked past his shoulder. "Is that a bag of chips I spot?"

"Um sure, you want some?"

"Dude, hand it over before I starve to death. I barely had time for breakfast."

"Do you want to come in?"

JP clamored in through the window. "Thought you'd never ask."

Two cans of Sprite and several bags of chips later, JP and Mars were sitting on the floor next to each other.

"What's going on, JP?" Mars said. "Nothing makes sense anymore. Maybe Aurora and Jonas are fine and it's *me*. Maybe I'm better off in Cleveland. All I do is get everyone in trouble."

"Are you kidding? That's definitely not what you do." JP wiped the crumbs from their fingers. "Here's why. Every day I have to decide what I'm wearing. You think that's easy? It's not. I want to be *me*. So maybe it's the color orange. Or sweats. And a sparkly scarf, too. I like mixing it up, bro. Because maybe I'm not exactly one thing. Why do I have to choose?"

"You don't," Mars said. "That's what's cool about you, JP."

"Then at school, I have to keep reminding people— I'm not a she, I'm not a he, I'm a they! And every teacher, except for maybe Mr. Q, gets it wrong. But it's more than what pronoun I use. It's also, Who am I? Because every-body wants you to make choices. They want you to check boxes."

"Yeah," Mars said. "I hear you." When he had to fill out school forms, there were always spaces to write about his dad—name, occupation, contact info. And Mars always had to leave them blank. He hated that. If only his mom would tell him a few things, but his dad was one of those forbidden topics. "But I still think I'm the one getting everyone else into trouble."

"Keep listening, Mars. I have a point. Do you remember two years ago, when some people started calling me boy-girl? 'There goes JP—which bathroom are you going to use, boy-girl?'"

"Clyde, you mean," Mars said.

"Exacto. Then he and his loser friends started teasing Toothpick. Now, people can do whatever they want with me, but they don't mess with my friend. Remember the first week of school in fourth grade? We were in the cafeteria, and they started making fun of Toothpick. Do you remember that?"

Mars nodded. "Sure."

"And I'm getting so mad you know I'm going to cream Clyde any minute."

"You would have been expelled, JP. You'd already punched him in the face once."

"OK, so I really don't like being called boy-girl." Even now, JP bristled at the memory. In fourth grade, that's when Clyde Boofsky kicked in with all his evilness. It was like the birth of the Boof.

"And I didn't want you to get expelled," Mars said.

"Yeah. I know that's why you dropped that stink bomb in the middle of the cafeteria. I don't even know why you had that thing with you, Mars!"

Mars smiled. "Fourth-grade science project. Eggs, vinegar, milk. Seal in a mason jar for a week, and bingo—you have a stink bomb. Good thing I had it with me in my backpack."

"Well, it was smelliest science project *I've* ever smelled. A million lunch staff had to clean it up. Pandemonium everywhere. The Boof out of the picture. You did that to save me. I knew it then. I know it now." JP took a deep breath. "*That's* why I'm here, Mars. You take care of me. I'll do anything for you. You know that."

"I know," Mars said softly.

JP looked at him. "So what do we do now? About Aurora and Jonas?"

"You mean that?" Mars asked. "You'll help me?"

"You tell me."

Reaching under the bed, Mars pulled out the envelope JP had found in Jonas's closet.

"You still have that?"

"I hid it inside my shirt when the police came. It's just like the one I got from Pruitt Prep."

"And you think it's important."

"It's the only thing that makes sense. We have to find out. But . . . I need help."

"Well, duh. Look no further. You've got *us.*"

"But Caddie won't talk to me. I don't know where Toothpick is. And—"

JP jumped up. "Leave that to me. What we need is a plan, Stan."

"Who's Stan?"

JP rolled their eyes. "Get with the expressions, Mars."

For the next few minutes JP and Mars mapped out what they were doing next. Now they needed to talk to everyone else.

"You stay put until I give you the heads up," JP said. They opened the window and hurried down the steps of the fire escape until they got to the end and leaped to the ground. JP looked up to call out goodbye when there was a thud on the ground next to them. "What are you doing?" JP asked, surprised.

Mars stood up, brushing the dust from his hands. "If you're going, I'd better go, too."

"But you're suspended! You aren't supposed to be at school."

He shrugged. "I was never much for rules."

JP laughed. "Neither am I, bro."

From: dfagan@hgwellsmiddeschool.org
To: squartz@hgwellsmiddleschool.org
Date: Tuesday, October 20, 8:20 a.m.
Subject: One of your students has been suspended

Dear MR. QUARTZ,

If you are receiving this email, this means that one of
your students, MANU PATEL, has been SUSPENDED
from H. G. Wells for a period of 1 DAY starting
IMMEDIATELY. He will return to school on WEDNESDAY.
Until then, he is not permitted ON SCHOOL GROUNDS.

The student is responsible for making up ALL missed
assignments in your classroom DETENTION.

Remember, at H. G. Wells, our school motto is: "Every
Success for Every Child." Sometimes success means
DISCIPLINE.

Sincerely,
Dorena Fagan
Principal
H. G. Wells Middle School

∩

**JP and Mars wanted to meet everyone in the janitor closet,** but when they got to school, they discovered duct tape had been placed across the door in a big X, along with a sign that read: OUT OF SERVICE INDEFINITELY.

"Someone knows about our place," Mars said. He looked up at the tiny cameras lining the hallway. "They probably know that I'm here, too."

"Then we gotta hurry," JP said. "Let's find them quick."

Toothpick was easy enough. He was in woodshop building a barometer-clock out of maple. On a bathroom break, they pulled him aside and went over the plan.

"Affirmative," Toothpick said.

Getting to Caddie in chorus class was harder. It meant sneaking into the gym. Luckily everyone was singing loud enough to cover up the sound of the big door opening and closing as JP and Mars slipped inside and crawled under the bleachers where the students were standing and singing. But how to get Caddie's attention?

*'Tis the gift to be simple, 'tis the gift to be free,*
*'tis the gift to come down where you ought to be,*
*and when we find ourselves in the place just right,*
*'twill be in the valley of love and delight.*

But before they could figure out what to do, Caddie

sensed them and peered through the bleachers. "What are you guys doing there?" she whispered. "You're going to get me in trouble."

"Check your texts, Cads," Mars whispered. "We need your help."

Caddie's eyes flickered uncertainly from him to JP.

"We think we know where Aurora and Jonas are," JP said.

"But to get there, we *need* you," Mars said. "You're the one who makes sure I don't do anything stupid."

"And it's a stupid plan," JP pointed out.

"Mars, you have to go," Caddie whispered. "If my parents find out . . ."

"Mars Patel?" a familiar voice cut in. An annoying familiar voice.

Caddie groaned. "Geez, now Epica spotted you."

Epica was incredulous. "Is that perv trying to look up my skirt?"

"You're wearing jeans, Epica," Caddie said, exasperated.

"Cads, will you help?" Mars pleaded. "Will you check your phone? Remember: *ad astra*."

Caddie was getting frazzled. "I don't even remember what that means, and—"

"*I* know what it means," Epica said.

"How would you know?" Mars asked.

"I know lots of things," Epica said in that singsongy voice of hers. "Because I'm smarter."

"Take a hike, Epica," JP growled.

"Um, I think *you're* the ones about to take a hike," Epica said. "Mrs. Bradley, Caddie is getting interrupted by someone under the bleachers," she announced loudly.

The music stopped.

Mrs. Bradley's voice rang out. "Caddie? Who are you talking to? You missed your solo!"

"Fine, guys!" Caddie whispered, glaring at Epica. She straightened. "Sorry, Mrs. Bradley." She cleared her throat and sang, *"When true simplicity is gained, to bow and to bend we shan't be ashamed!"*

"Go, go!" JP urged while Caddie was singing and the music started up again. They bolted to the door.

"Is someone there?" Mrs. Bradley called out. "Now wait a minute! That's not—"

This time they rushed down the eighth-grade hall until they got to the double doors.

"That was close," JP said panting as they adjusted their orange scarf. "I almost lost my scarf back there. Not cool."

"Tonight, nine o'clock," Mars said. "I'll text everyone. I hope Caddie comes."

"Oh, she will," JP said. "Caddie's our girl."

"Mars? What are you doing in school?" Mr. Q stood behind them, dressed in one of his usual plaid shirts, the frames of his glasses dark against his pale face. "You're suspended."

"Please don't tell anyone," Mars pleaded. "We think we know how to find Jonas and Aurora. But we have to do it together. As a team."

Would Mr. Q rat them out? He was carrying a bag of bird seed and garden shears, headed for the front lawn. He was the only one who cared about the birds and the hedges. And them. "Go," he said. "I never saw either of you."

Mars flashed a grateful look and disappeared through the double doors.

"You're the best, Mr. Q," JP said. "I'd hug you, but yo, I'm not the type."

He smiled faintly. "Noted."

Hey there, listeners, do you want to succeed
but you don't know how?
Each year, students around the world
take my GIFT test to get into
the most prestigious school on the planet:
Pruitt Prep!

Want some extra help?
Visit www.pruittprep.com.
With study guides, practice tests,
and tips from real PP students,
taking the GIFT doesn't need to be a mystery.

PRUITT PREP: TO THE STARS!

500 Comments ⊗

godzilla   60 min ago
the GIFT is in 2 days yikessssss

wormhole   50 min ago
anyone hear about the missing kids in texas? #missingkids

lostinlondon   41 min ago
on it #missingkids

oreocookies   23 min ago
What's a GIFT

allie_j   22 min ago
OMG what planet are you on?????

oreocookies   21 min ago
haha just kidding

# 9

# THE PLAN, STAN

**Mars · Caddie · JP · Toothpick**

Tues, Oct 20, 12:03 pm

Mars
We meet 9 sharp @ dock – JP carries water and food supplies

JP
Will do

Mars
Pick print a map of school plus anything else useful

Toothpick
Roger that

Mars
Caddie u in

Caddie
Ya I'm in

JP

yayyyyy

Toothpick

Second that

Mars

Cads thank you!!!

Caddie

What do u need from me

Mars

rest your mind we need it to spot danger

Caddie

what danger

Mars

Wear dark clothes don't tell anyone

Caddie

Do u think we'll find them

Toothpick

We won't know until we try

JP

let's rock this mission

Mars

Oh ya delete these texts

Mars

We made a plan

To come get u and jonas

like maybe in a few hours

the whole mystery will b solved

and I'll find u

u know u can count on me right

a promise is a promise

# 10

# GALE ISLAND

**C**addie knew Mars was right about Gale Island. She hadn't told him or anyone, but the island was pulling at her. It had been pulling at her for a long time. She didn't know whether they would find Aurora and Jonas there. But now that they were all going, she knew they would find *something*.

She also found that getting out of her second floor bedroom window was easier this time. On her climb down the trellis, she jumped to the right of the rosebush. There was a fine mist in the air when Caddie got on her bike, and the night smelled sweet. She could almost taste it, the sweetness, and then something unexpected happened—she started to feel *excited*. By the time she got to the dock, it was full-out raining which was fine since she was wearing her raincoat (she'd checked the forecast), and she was literally shaking with excitement. The pulling feeling was getting stronger with every minute.

Toothpick and JP were already there. Toothpick was wearing a coat, too, and some kind of vest with a bunch of gadgets and equipment inside all the pockets. He called it his survival gear. Meanwhile, JP was getting drenched.

"I HATE being wet," JP whined.

Toothpick offered to make a raincoat out of an empty trash bag in his backpack.

"No, thanks," JP said. "I don't need to be garbage. Where's Mars?"

"I'm here." Mars pulled up on his bike. "Sorry I'm late. I was checking the ferry schedule. It comes at nine o'clock. Which is like—"

"Three minutes ago," Toothpick said. "But there's no sign of a ferry."

Mars peered into the dark water. "Why is there no ferry? The schedule says there's supposed to be one."

"Well, there is a boat," Toothpick added slowly. "A small boat."

Mars brightened. "OK, now we're talking."

"Hold on," JP said. "I thought we were getting to Gale Island on a ferry. A ferry is a whole lot bigger than a boat. Did I mention I hate getting wet?"

Caddie sighed. "Mars, we don't even know what kind of boat," she said.

Toothpick led everyone to the edge of the shore. A small boat bobbed in the water, tied to a cleat on the dock with a piece of rope. In the dark it was hard to tell whose boat it was or what shape it was in.

JP bunched up their fists like they were going to deck someone. "*That's it?* That's the boat?"

Mars looked at Caddie. "Are you getting any bad vibes, Cads?"

She looked out over the water. The pulling feeling was even stronger here at the shore. But before she could say anything, JP butted in.

"What about me?" JP fumed. "*I'm* getting bad vibes. Listen, Mars, I've gone along with everything else. But me getting in that puny boat? NO WAY. Because if you don't know by now, I HATE BEING WET."

Caddie's eyes met Mars's.

Five minutes later, cold and wet, they were in the row-boat to Gale Island.

∩

**The rain made plinking sounds as they rowed across the** inky water. No one could see except Toothpick, who was using his flashlight to look at his compass and say which way to go. Meanwhile Caddie and JP were stuck rowing as

Mars listened to his podcast, and Toothpick kept getting up to peer ahead.

"Pick, sit or you'll capsize the boat!" JP growled. "Ugh, I can't believe we're in this boat."

"My compass works better when I'm standing," Toothpick said. "Head due north."

"I don't know which way north is," Caddie said. The rain was making her glasses foggy. "But I think I know where to go."

"By the way, I'm still wet!" JP called out. "Sit down, Pick, or I swear I'll strangle you. And Mars, stop listening to that podcast. I'm strong, but I can't be the only one rowing."

"I'm rowing too," Caddie said. "And we're veering too far to the left."

"Wow, Caddie is better than my compass," Toothpick said, sitting down finally.

"We're veering," JP seethed, "because somebody is on his phone instead of rowing."

Toothpick stood up again. "Yeah, we're still veering."

"You don't get it. I *need* to listen to the podcast," Mars said. "Sometimes Oliver Pruitt . . ." he hesitated. "Sometimes he gives clues."

"Are you serious?" JP asked.

Caddie could feel the knot in Mars's stomach. She was feeling one in her stomach, too. Was that pulling she felt from Gale Island a good thing or not? It was hard to tell with everyone bickering. "Oliver did say something big would happen," she said to everyone, "right before the Code Red."

"And remember," Mars said, "that's when Jonas disappeared."

"Next you'll say he *made* that Code Red happen," JP muttered.

"Oliver Pruitt giving us clues on his podcast," Toothpick mused, "means he is observing our every move. Which means he would need highly specialized satellite technology."

"Listen, everyone," JP said. "I hate to break this to you, but Oliver Pruitt is *not* watching us. He's got a massive empire and a buttload of smart kids in his school. He's not interested in a bunch of delinquents from H. G. Wells drowning in the middle of Puget Sound."

The boat tottered wildly.

"Pick, sit down!" JP and Mars shouted at the same time.

"Stop it, all of you!" Caddie glared at everyone. "Don't you see? We're all we've got," she said. "We can't be fighting with each other. It's not normal that Aurora and Jonas are gone without a trace. Mars is right. And whoever is responsible could be after one of us next."

There was a pause. Caddie could feel the tension softening around her. JP stopped thinking about the ham sandwich in the fridge back home. Toothpick stopped trying to get the compass to work and tried to trust his friends instead. And Mars? Would he ever stop thinking about Oliver Pruitt? At least it had stopped raining.

"Gosh, Cads," JP said. "I'm sorry."

"Me, too," Toothpick said. "You're right. The boat is progressing in the right direction."

"Thanks, Cads," Mars murmured, putting his phone in his coat pocket. *You balance us out.* He didn't say the words, but she could feel them.

"You're welcome," Caddie said. Just then the bottom of the boat scraped the shore. "Good timing," she said. "Because we just reached Gale Island."

# 11
## WHERE IS IT?

**A**s soon as everyone got out, they looked for a place to tie the boat.

"How about the dock?" JP said. The dock was a narrow set of planks jutting out from the shore with GALE ISLAND on a sign so small it would be easy to miss.

Mars nodded. "On the count of three, let's all pull—" Before he could finish, JP had already grabbed the end and dragged the boat forward.

JP grinned. "That felt good. Anybody else got stuff to haul?"

After the boat was tied, Toothpick distributed flashlights to everyone. Then he unrolled his map. He hadn't been sure his phone would work on the island, so he'd printed it out.

"Good idea," Mars said. "My connection is dead."

"Mine, too," JP said. "You'd think Pruitt Prep would offer free Wi-Fi."

"So what does your map say?" Caddie asked.

They crowded around as Toothpick explained everything. "See, we go through the woods here. That gets us to the front of Pruitt Prep. These are the science towers and the botany lab. This is the titanium wall surrounding the school. By the way, titanium is strong and highly durable, one of the strongest metals known, used for airplanes, but also for toothpaste."

"Toothpaste! How do you know all this stuff?" JP asked.

"I'm not really sure," Toothpick said. "How did you drag the boat up on shore?"

"What does my strength have to do with your brain?" JP asked.

"I guess it's just who we are," Toothpick said. He rolled up the map. "Let's go."

"Let's stick together, too, Pick," Mars called out as he saw Toothpick disappear ahead through a thicket of trees.

"Don't worry. I'll keep an eye on him," JP said as they followed Toothpick, weaving between twiggy pine trees that seemed to be everywhere. Then JP flexed their arms in and out curiously. "Guys, am I the only one, or does it feel like there's something different here?"

"Yeah," Mars said. "Though I'm not sure why."

Caddie's teeth chattered. "One thing: it's really cold. Brr."

"You're shivering, girl," JP said. "Here, take my sweatshirt."

Caddie tried to say no. "I thought you hated being wet."

"That's wet. I can handle cold." JP removed their Arsenal sweatshirt and gave it to Caddie. "Here. It's not even wet anymore for some reason. It should keep you nice and toasty."

"Thanks, JP." Caddie took the sweatshirt gratefully and put it on under her raincoat. "I don't know why I'm so c-c-old. Guess I'm just sensitive." The sweatshirt felt warm and smelled like cinnamon. JP had baked cinnamon cookies in the morning to cheer themself up. It was hard to imagine JP sad, but it must have been because of that thing JP's mom said, about not wearing such crazy clothes all the time. That memory was still fresh in JP's mind, and Caddie was surprised by how quickly she could sense it.

"But I love the way you dress," Caddie said, then stopped, realizing JP hadn't said anything.

JP laughed. "Well, don't think you're keeping my Arsenal sweatshirt or anything."

As they continued through the woods, a sound came in the distance. Was it . . . a howl? It came again. Then another time.

JP stopped. "Guuuuys . . . what was that?"

"It sounds like . . . a wolf," Mars said slowly. Were there wolves in Puget Sound?

There it was again. Only now it was getting louder. And it sounded like a growl.

Mars swallowed. "Let's hurry up, all right? And make some noise."

"So it knows where to find us?" JP shot back. "Sorry, I don't want to be wolf food."

"Mars is right," Caddie said. "When I went hiking in Alaska last year, we had bells in our hands to ring in case a bear came by. The noise scares them away. You should know that, JP. Didn't you go to Alaska one summer?"

"Maybe I missed Bells 101," JP said.

Meanwhile, Mars pulled out the headphone jack and turned up the volume so everyone could listen along to the podcast he had downloaded to his phone earlier in the afternoon.

*Listeners, a puzzle for you.*
*A man goes upstairs to get his time machine.*
*He walks back downstairs,*
*and he travels back in time two hundred years.*
*Why did he go downstairs first?*
*Hint: HEAD FOR THE CLEARING.*

"Oh man, not Oliver Pruitt," JP groaned.

Behind them the howling sound came again.

"It's a good distraction," Mars said. "Why does the man go back down the stairs, JP?"

"No clue," JP said. "Maybe he needed a sandwich. I sure could use one."

Behind them, the howling sounded even closer. And it was gaining!

"OK, guys, RUN!" Mars shouted.

They bolted through the thick underbrush. There was no time to think whether they were going in the right direction. Whatever was howling was getting closer. Now they could hear it plowing through the trees, tearing across the wooded ground. Mars thought of deer being hunted and wondered if this was what it felt like. Except, were *they* the deer?

"Faster!" Mars yelled. There was a clearing up ahead. Suddenly OP's words came hurtling back. "We need to get to the clearing," he shouted. "We'll be safe there."

"How do you know?" Caddie yelled behind him.

"He doesn't," JP yelled back. "Let's do it anyway."

There was no more time for talking, just running while whatever it was chased them, howling and gnashing its teeth.

"Keep going!" Mars yelled. "Don't stop!"

A few minutes later they broke through the woods and stumbled into the clearing, which was a large, open field. Everyone stopped to catch their breath.

"It's gone," Caddie said as she gulped air. "I don't feel it anymore."

"You could feel it, Caddie?" JP asked, breathing hard. "Like how you can feel us thinking?"

She shook her head. "No, I could *sense* it. It went back where it came from. It didn't want to be in the clearing."

"That's what the podcast said," Mars said. "Remember?"

JP shook their head. "I didn't hear anything. Sorry, I was too busy running for my life."

"How could Oliver know we'd be near a clearing at this hour?" Mars wondered. He suddenly noticed something else. "And where's Pick?"

"He's not here," Caddie whispered. "I don't sense him."

"This can't be happening," JP moaned. "We can't lose Pick, too."

Mars's heart started beating. How many of his friends were going to disappear? Did the thing that was chasing them . . . get Pick?

"I hope not, Mars," Caddie said softly.

Mars looked at her. "I didn't say anything," he said.

Just then, JP called out. "Look, guys, there he is. Up ahead! Pick! Pick!"

They ran to him. Mars was so relieved to see him. Then he saw his face.

"What's wrong?" Mars asked breathlessly. "Are you OK? Did you get hurt?"

Toothpick shook his head. "I'm fine. I just don't understand it. It can't be," he murmured.

"What, Pick?" Mars asked.

"I watched the videos," he said. "I studied the layout. I know it all by heart. The science towers, the botany lab, the virtual-reality auditorium, the café with the living roof." He pointed to his map. "*This* is where it's supposed to be. But look—it's gone."

"*What's* gone?" JP asked.

Toothpick gestured to the dark, empty field ahead of them.

"Pruitt Prep," he said.

♩

**"Maybe the school is on some other part of the island,"** Caddie said.

"And we came to the wrong part?" JP asked. The twigs on the ground made snapping sounds as everyone tromped back through the dark woods toward the shore. By now, the howling thing, whatever it was, had thankfully disappeared.

"The map I downloaded seemed accurate," Toothpick

said. "And I cross-checked the coordinates with Google Maps."

"What if there's no school?" JP said.

"You mean it's a fake location?" asked Toothpick.

JP shrugged. "There are worse things."

"I agree with Mars," Caddie said.

"I didn't say anything," Mars said. "Again."

"Oh," Caddie said.

"The school is real," Mars said.

"Yeah, like I said, I agree with Mars," Caddie said again.

"That's because he likes Oliver Pruitt," JP said. "Makes sense."

"Look at all the stuff online," Mars said. "The website, the YouTube videos, the interviews. And the brochure. You can't take pictures of a fake school."

"You'd be surprised," JP said.

"Oliver Pruitt is a rich billionaire," Caddie asked. "Why would he have a fake school?"

"Why would he take our friends?" JP asked pointedly.

"We don't know that he did," Toothpick said. "That's just speculation."

JP flapped their arms out in the dark. "Then why are we here? Mars thinks Jonas and Aurora are at Pruitt Prep. They can't be here unless Oliver Pruitt had something to do with it."

As they continued walking, Mars looked up at the night

sky. Somewhere Oliver was transmitting his podcast every day. All along, Mars had assumed it was from Pruitt Prep. But Pruitt Prep wasn't here. Was it all a trick? But why would the greatest mind in the world be bothered with fooling the four of them? Not to mention the thousands of other kids listening to his podcast?

And now this trip to Gale Island had been a complete waste of time. He had let his friends down. He'd sent Aurora that text. If she'd got it, she thought he was on the way, just like she'd thought her dad was on the way. And just like her dad, Mars had failed her.

He sighed. Either he was confused or just plain dumb.

"You're not dumb, Mars," Caddie said. "Stop blaming yourself. And Toothpick can stop blaming his map. He didn't put it up on the Web; Oliver Pruitt did."

Toothpick looked at her. "I didn't say anything."

"And there's no food here either, JP," Caddie added. "So you can stop thinking about that."

Everyone stared at her.

Caddie stopped. "Am I doing that thing again?"

"You're in all of our minds," Toothpick observed. "At the same time. It's unprecedented."

"And annoying," JP said.

"I'm sorry," Caddie said softly. "I'm not trying to be. And I don't know where the school went, Mars! Stop thinking I'd know."

She walked off.

"What got into her?" JP wondered. "Just because I was hungry?"

∩

**Mars hurried to catch up with Caddie.**

"Cads, is everything OK?" he asked. "You seem . . . upset."

"I'm fine," she said without looking at him. "I just needed some space. So many thoughts, and they're not even mine!"

"Oh," Mars said.

They walked in silence, the sound of the ground crunching under their feet. Autumn in Port Elizabeth was gloomy and wet, and all you wanted to do was stay home and drink hot chocolate and watch a movie. Mars felt like that now, like wanting to be some place dry and warm. As for the movie . . . well, his life felt like a movie. Just not in a good way.

Caddie was shivering again. Mars offered his coat, but she shook her head as she rubbed her hands together. He could see her breaths coming out in white puffs, which was odd because he couldn't see his own breath.

Everything seemed so complicated. The only thing that made sense was Caddie. Without her, he wouldn't have come to Gale Island; he wouldn't have broken into Jonas's house; he wouldn't keep looking for their friends. There were a lot of things Mars wouldn't do without Caddie. He wished he could make her feel better the way she did for him.

"I guess I've gotten used to other people's feelings," Caddie said. "It was hard when I was little. So many mean people, Mars. With such mean feelings."

"Yeah," Mars said. "Like in first grade, it made you cry."

"It's different here," Caddie said. "I can read *actual* thoughts, not just sense them. I can be completely inside everyone's minds. Like poor Toothpick. He's feeling terrible about not finding the school. He always gets things right. It's huge with him. Now he's close to tears, even though he can't tell anyone that. And JP? You think they're all tough, but they get worried and scared, too. JP had a fight with their mom this morning, and JP wonders if they'll ever be accepted in this world."

"JP shouldn't care what anybody thinks."

"JP doesn't let anybody know they care. Except there I am, inside their head. It's crazy! And wrong, too."

"So you mean you can tell what *everyone* is thinking?" Mars asked. He stopped walking. Caddie did, too. "Then what am I thinking right now?" he asked curiously. And just like that, a thought popped in his mind before he could stop it. He didn't even know it was there until it was.

"Oh, Mars," she said. "If you want to ask me to the dance, you should."

"Wait," Mars said, his face heating up. He didn't know

how that idea had crept into his head. Maybe it had been there all this time, but it confused him because wasn't he looking for Aurora, too?

"I don't know how Aurora would feel about it, either," Caddie said softly, "but I imagine she's got other things to worry about at this moment."

"You're right. I mean," he said, flustered, "about wanting to ask you, that is. So, uh . . . would you go to the dance with me, Caddie? Like, if we get home and there aren't more disasters?"

He couldn't tell in the dark, but he thought Caddie smiled. "I would love to go," she said.

"Awesome," Mars said. Wow, it was weird that he had to be on Gale Island to ask her.

"Yeah, it is weird," Caddie agreed. Then she stopped. "Sorry, I'll try not to do that, even though it's basically impossible."

By now, JP and Toothpick had reached them. "Listen folks, let's keep it moving. Toothpick, do you remember where we tied the boat?"

"Yes, it's this way," Toothpick said. "The shore is right there."

A few minutes later they reached the beach and stared into the rippling waters.

And they discovered a bigger problem.

The rickety rowboat they had tied to the dock was gone.

There was nothing left behind except the moonless night. And them.

JP was furious. "I tied the boat, didn't I? Tell me I'm not crazy." In their hand JP squeezed their flashlight in frustration and suddenly it buckled under their grip. "Oops," JP said.

Toothpick pushed up his glasses. "You're not crazier than the rest of us, JP. Though maybe you shouldn't be handling any more flashlights." He took the mangled flashlight from JP and put it in his backpack.

"I'm sorry, Pick. I don't know my own strength," JP said. "But that still doesn't tell me why the boat I dragged over here and tied up has vanished."

Toothpick nodded. "Agree. Either a person or an animal was responsible for untying it."

"You mean the wolf?" JP crossed their arms then leaned forward. "And now I can't see a blinking *thing*. Somebody got a light?"

Toothpick rifled through his backpack.

Meanwhile, Mars was thinking about what Toothpick had said. He was right. That boat didn't get loose on its own. So who untied it? A *wolf*? Someone from Pruitt Prep? Oliver? As Mars was trying to figure it out, JP caught on fire.

## 12
# WHAT THE BLAZES?

When JP had crushed their flashlight like an empty soda can, their own strength stunned JP momentarily. But mostly they were annoyed it was so dark. When JP asked for a light, they assumed Toothpick would hand out another flashlight from his backpack filled with every kind of survival equipment you could imagine. Instead he pulled out an Ultimate Survival Match. When lit, it was capable of withstanding rain, sleet, and hail. Or something like that. Toothpick had told JP about the matches while they were still in Port Elizabeth waiting for Caddie and Mars to come. Nothing puts them out, he'd said. Nothing.

When JP lit one, it gave a fabulous flame. They'd never seen anything so bright from a single matchstick.

"Dude!" JP said appreciatively. "That *is* ultimate!" But

before they could tell Toothpick just how epic the match was, JP tripped over a large branch in their path.

Then everyone started screaming.

"JP! Your shirt!" Caddie yelled.

"Quick, roll on the ground!" Toothpick shouted next.

Then Mars tackled JP onto the sand with his jacket.

"Oof," JP said, tumbling down.

"What's everyone getting in a tizzy for?" JP asked, standing up.

Toothpick breathed, "JP, you were combusting."

"What?"

"On fire," Mars said plainly. "You were on fire."

"Didn't you feel it?" Caddie wondered. "You didn't, did you? You have no idea what we're talking about. And will you stop thinking about food for a second? You almost got killed!"

It took them a few minutes to sort it out. That JP had been literally on fire, until Mars snuffed them out. But the bigger thing, more than being a human candle, was that JP didn't feel any of it.

"Well, I am kind of strong . . ." JP said slowly.

"Are you kidding?" Caddie said. "Strength has nothing to do with that."

"It's as if JP was fireproof," Toothpick speculated. "Able to withstand great heat."

JP grinned. "All right. Now we're talking. Like I'm a superhero or something." JP looked out at the dark water and paused. "But, um, guys . . . how do we get home?"

∩

**Toothpick knew what to do.**

"We build a fire," he said. Everyone looked immediately at JP. "Not like that," he added quickly. "Like, a real fire. To keep us warm. And to send an SOS."

"Who are we SOSing out there?" JP asked.

"The Marines. The National Guard."

"Really?" JP's voice went up.

"Or pretty much anyone on a boat," Toothpick said. He told everyone to collect firewood and kindling. "We need small, thin sticks. Dead and dry. Look for them on the trees. Coniferous are the best. Anything on the ground will be damp."

They split into two groups, with Mars and Caddie going off near the woods to collect bigger branches while Toothpick and JP and built a shelter on the beach for the fire.

"I still don't get how you know all this," JP said as they gathered driftwood for the shelter. "No offense, but you aren't exactly Boy Scout material."

"I know," Toothpick agreed. "I do have a good memory. Only . . . it seems even better here."

"That's what I said," JP agreed. "Something about being here, I guess." JP dropped a large branch on the ground that almost landed on Toothpick's feet before he leaped out of the way.

Toothpick cleared his throat. "Maybe not so big, JP?"

"Sorry, Pick!"

Toothpick got out some twine to tie together the smaller pieces of driftwood. "Still, it's my fault we didn't find the school. That's why we came. And I let you all down."

"Let us down?" JP repeated. "You had the map. You knew the way. That's why you went ahead of us, remember? We were worried when we didn't see you."

Toothpick set down the twine. "Twine is important. The best tactical survival kits include it. As well as equipment to skin a wild animal, collect tree sap, and take out splinters."

"Hmm," JP said. "Like, I have no idea why you're telling me all that, but OK."

"But the most important thing is a map," he said. "So you were worried about not having the map. That's why you were worried when you didn't see me."

"Wait," JP said, "you think we needed you because of your map?"

"Wouldn't that make sense?"

"No, Pick," JP said, shaking their head. "We were worried about YOU."

"Oh," he said. For a moment he didn't say anything. "You were worried about me?"

"That's right, Pick. YOU."

He pushed up his glasses. "You worry a lot about me," he said slowly. "Like at school. You don't like it if someone picks on me."

"'Course not. You're my bro. No one messes with my bro."

Toothpick nodded. "That word, *bro*—you use it when you want to call someone cool, hip, or a good friend."

JP rolled their eyes. "Not if you put it that way. Like, maybe I gotta stop using *bro* now."

"It's hard for me to use the word *bro*," Toothpick said seriously.

"So don't. Hand me some of that twine, will you?"

Toothpick reached down to pass the ball of twine. He was struggling to say something, but he didn't know how to get it out.

"Pick, are you OK?" JP asked. "Listen, I get it. You don't have to say *bro*."

"You don't have to worry. I can take care of myself. But thank you . . . for worrying about me."

JP smiled, then fake punched him on the shoulder. "That's what friends do."

"I'm feeling something," he said. "Goodwill, I think. And friendship. Like cotton candy inside of me."

JP smirked. "I *think* that's a compliment, but I'm not sure."

Together they tied all the ends until they had finally built a driftwood shelter.

"This is real good, Pick!" JP said. "You rock."

Toothpick grinned. "Or you could say, I drift!"

JP groaned. "Bad pun alert."

When Mars and Caddie came back with the firewood and kindling, Toothpick showed everyone how to build a hearth inside the shelter. "This will trap the heat. We need to do that to keep the fire lit."

"Dude," JP said. "Is there nothing you don't know?"

A few minutes later they had a roaring fire thanks to the hearth and the Ultimate Survival Matches.

"Do you think the SOS will work?" Mars asked. "Like, who will see the fire and come?"

"It will work," Toothpick said simply. "It worked on *Frontier Living*."

"That's a show, Pick," JP pointed out.

"It's the most realistic survival show on TV," he said.

"So guys, are we now, like, missing kids?" JP asked.

"You mean like the ones around the world?" Toothpick asked. "I keep reading about them."

"Yeah, the podcast was talking about the missing kids in the comments, too," Mars said.

"Maybe they went missing because they were looking for their friends," Caddie wondered.

"Great," JP said. "That's so reassuring, since *that's what we're doing right now.* Time for some happy thoughts, folks." JP pulled out the chips from their backpack and handed them out.

Everyone sat around the fire, munching on chips and wondering what would happen next.

"Isn't it strange how here on this island everybody's like . . . more?" Mars asked. "JP is more strong. Toothpick is more smart. Caddie is more able to read our minds."

"Are you implying that the island is giving us heightened skills?" Toothpick asked. "I do feel more alert. I can remember better. Build better. Reason better. Maybe you're onto something."

"I know exactly what you mean," JP said. "I'm stronger than ever, I'm not getting hurt, and you know something else? It's wet and windy and I should be cold, but I'm not."

Caddie nodded, her teeth chattering again. "Speak for yourself. I'm freezing even with your sweatshirt on. But maybe I'm more sensitive to cold on the island?" She looked at Mars. "And you're more, too."

Mars looked startled. "Stop doing that, Cads. I'm fine."

"I know what you're thinking," she said.

"What's he thinking?" JP asked.

"That he isn't sure what he's doing for all of us," Caddie said. "But that's not the way friends think, right?"

"You're doing plenty," JP said.

"You have been single-minded in locating our friends," Toothpick said. "We are on a difficult mission. We need a good leader."

"You're a good leader," Caddie said.

"Geez," Mars said, embarrassed. "You don't have to say all that. I'm the one who dragged you out here. And . . ." He sighed. "Sometimes I don't even know what I'm doing anymore."

A few moments later there came a pinging sound from Mars's phone. A text notification.

"I thought phones didn't work here," Caddie said.

"Me, too," Mars said. "Who sent this?"

Everyone leaned over him to read the text as he held up his phone.

---

**Mars · LIL**

Tues, Oct 20, 11:34 pm

LIL (Lost in London)
**You're not alone**

---

"LIL?" JP repeated.

"Maybe the person meant to write LOL," Toothpick guessed.

"But this is Lost in London, Pick," JP said. "That's what LIL stands for."

"Who's LIL, Mars?" Caddie asked.

"I have no idea." He looked out toward the water. "Hey, you guys. I see something."

"I don't see anything at all," JP said. "Are you sure, Mars?"

Toothpick took out a pair of binoculars from his survival pack. "He's right. It's a boat!"

"Oh, Toothpick, your fire worked!" Caddie said. "And you know what? I can feel the boat now. It's heading our way."

"Who is it? The National Guard?" he asked. "They're responsible for rescue missions."

"I'm not sure. But it's coming for us. And . . ." Caddie held her fingers up to her forehead. "It's someone we know!"

"I hope it isn't my parents," Toothpick said immediately.

"What if it's Oliver Pruitt?" Mars wondered.

"Calling Earth to Mars," JP said. "Oliver Pruitt isn't thinking about us."

Now they could hear the puttering of a motorboat. Closer and closer it came until the outline of the boat was in view. Whoever it was killed the engine. They shone their remaining flashlights to see who it was.

"Look, it's Mr. Q!" Toothpick called out.

Mr. Q held his hand up to shield the light from his eyes.

"Why am I not surprised?" he asked. "I should have guessed it would be you guys."

They spent the next few minutes putting out the fire

on the beach by dumping sand over it. With all of them working, it didn't take long. Then one by one, Mr. Q helped them onto his boat.

When they were in the boat and seated, Mr. Q gave them all life vests to wear.

"Are we glad you came when you did," JP said to Mr. Q.

"Had enough of Gale Island, have you?" Mr. Q asked.

"Well, yeah," JP said. "From Toothpick's extra braininess to Caddie reading minds, to me being fireproof, I think I had enough for one night. Not to mention that the sch—"

"How did you even find us?" Mars interrupted loudly.

JP stopped talking, but when Mr. Q looked away to steer the boat, they mouthed *What?* to Mars. He just shook his head back.

"I saw your fire," Mr. Q was saying, "and thought I would check it out. Looks like it was a good decision." He smiled, the wind sending his hair into peaks. "The weather is getting nasty and the last thing you want is to be stuck on an island in Puget Sound."

"What were you doing on the sound at this hour?" Mars asked. His voice was flat.

"Oh, this and that," Mr. Q said. "It's how I get my thoughts clear—going out on the water at night, observing marine life. Sometimes I see harbor seals and otters swimming in the moonlight."

"But there's no moon," Mars said. "Seems like a big coincidence, you being here."

"What, Mars? Would you rather I *hadn't* found you tonight?" Mr. Q said it good-naturedly, but Mars could sense a sudden sharpness in his voice.

"No, of course not," Mars said immediately. He glanced at his phone. "Oh look, I'm getting a signal finally."

"Yeah all my bars," JP said. "Time to check messages."

Mr. Q looked at them, mildly amused. "Can't be without your phones, can you, kids?"

He continued steering the boat as they all scrolled through their messages. Meanwhile, Mars started texting.

| Mars · JP · Toothpick · Caddie |
|---|

Wed, Oct 21, 12:18 am

Mars
**Isn't it strange Mr Q just showed up at this hour**

JP
**Who cares he rescued us**

Toothpick
**He is an expert boater notice how he handles the waves**

Mars
**Cads are you getting any bad vibes**

Caddie
**No it's Mr Q he's always helping us**

Toothpick
**Why**

**Are u worried**

JP
**Try paranoid**

Mars
**Let's not tell him anything about why we were on Gale**

Caddie
**U think he's not being straight with us**

Mars
**Not sure**


Mr. Q glanced at everyone. "Strap in, kids," he called from the helm. "It's going to be a bumpy ride home." Then he guided the boat into the dark waters, heading back to Port Elizabeth.

## Mars · Aurora

Wed, Oct 21, 1:23 am

Mars
**aurora where is Pruitt Prep**

**And where r u??**

From: dfagan@hgwellsmiddeschool.org
To: staff@hgwellsmiddleschool.org
Date: Thursday, October 22, 8:15 a.m.
Subject: Assembly Today

Dear FACULTY AND STAFF,

In anticipation of this week's GIFT test, there will be a special assembly held in the gymnasium at 11 a.m. TODAY. Please have your students ready. Also ensure that ALL CELL PHONES, HANDHELD DEVICES, BACKPACKS, and LARGE BAGS are left behind. None of these will be permitted in the gymnasium, as requested by our special presenter. Students will also be required to go through security clearance, following our new security and safety protocols.

Our speaker promises to be a source of inspiration for students and faculty alike. I promise you an assembly like no other! Remember, at H. G. Wells, our school motto is: "Every Success for Every Child." Sometimes success means COOPERATION. Reiterate: NO CELL PHONES.

Sincerely,
Dorena Fagan
Principal
H. G. Wells Middle School

# H. G. Wells Middle School

## MEMO

**DATE: OCT. 22**
**TO: H. G. WELLS BUILDING PERSONNEL**
**FROM: S. QUARTZ**

Microphone, stereo system, and surround sound required in gym for special assembly. Please ensure all systems working and in place. Sound check at 10:45 a.m.

15 ▶ 30

Dear listeners, true story here.

When I was a child, an astronaut came to talk to our school.

He told us about gravity and rocket fuel and how nothing travels faster than light through the vacuum of space.

I was very intrigued.

So in front of the entire school, I asked him:

"Can you send a message on a beam of light through space?"

And guess what? Everyone laughed at me!

But even as a boy, I knew it was possible.

I knew it was just a matter of thinking differently.

You know what else travels at the speed of light?

Thoughts. Feelings. Imagination.

I look at our world now, and I don't like what I see

We are not taking care of our planet.

We're not taking care of the people living on it, either.

We need another option.

But to create one, we need kids with
imagination and courage.

Kids brave enough to start something different and new.

Will that be you leading the way?

Say YES in the comments section
if you're ready to imagine the future with me.

**2000 Comments** ⊗

godzilla  30 min ago
love this YES

toadstool  27 min ago
YES

jerseyshores  25 min ago
YYYYY

neptunebaby  24 min ago
YES

allie_j  18 min ago
yeah!

staryoda  15 min ago
yesssss

thisismars  14 min ago
yes

dreamship  11 min ago
yes

moonbeam  9 min ago
yes!!!!

wormhole  8 min ago
missing kids reported in florida too #missingkids

galaxygenius  7 min ago
maybe it's the flu everyone's home sick

galaxygenius  6 min ago
yesss to OP's qtn

allie_j  5 min ago
do we still need to take GIFT if we say yes

lostinlondon  4 min ago
yayyy #wingsofscience #futureishere

wormhole  1 min ago
NOT THE FLU #missingkids

# 13
# THE WINGS OF SCIENCE

Oliver's last podcast was the most awesome one Mars had ever heard. It even gave him goose bumps. A beam of light, imagining the future . . . Mars could think of nothing else as he walked to the assembly.

"Mars, thank God," Caddie said when she saw him in front of the gym. "I'm glad I found someone I know. You know how I hate assemblies. Too many people. All their feelings flying around gives me a headache."

"I thought you block them out," Mars said as he stuck his phone in his pocket.

"I do. But it's like there's a door and they're all waiting on the other side."

Mars grinned. "Then don't open the door, Cads."

"Thanks," Caddie said, rolling her eyes. "I'll try to remember that."

Mars remembered their conversation on the island. Had he really asked her to the dance? He'd never asked a girl to anything. And she'd said yes! He wondered if she could read his mind now. If she was, she wasn't acting like it. *Just be yourself*, he thought. Whatever that meant.

They spotted JP and Toothpick in the bleachers and joined them.

"Like I said, Pick, hit me right here," JP said, indicating a place on their chin.

"You want me to hit you as hard as I can?" Toothpick asked doubtfully.

"Remember last night on the island when I caught on fire?" JP asked. "I'm indestructible. Now I want to prove it. Punch me in the face."

"OK," Toothpick said agreeably. "But just so you know, I forgot the bus schedule this morning. I'm not remembering everything like I did last night."

Caddie scrunched her face. "I can't read your minds, either!" she said. Her eyes flickered to Mars and she flushed. "Well, um, not like yesterday."

"OK, JP," Toothpick said, pulling back a fist. "Get ready, because—"

"On second thought, let's wait," JP said quickly. They noticed Mars's distracted expression. "What's wrong, Mars?"

"I'm not sure," Mars said. He frowned, his eyes on the

stage. "Mr. Q is down there. And he's giving me a look."

"I see him," Caddie said. "And . . . ow." She reached to hold her head with her fingers. "Mars . . . Now I'm feeling something, too."

"It's just everyone around us, Cads," JP said. "You getting their feels, girl?"

Caddie shook her head. "I can block that. This is more like something's"—she looked at the stage, puzzled—"there."

"*Mr. Q* is there," JP said. "Even I can see that."

Everyone watched as Mr. Q ran a sound check on the stage. Suddenly there was a loud hum in the air.

"Whoa, did the lights just flicker?" JP wondered.

"That's a sixty-cycle hum," Toothpick said. "I don't know what they're doing, but whatever they're plugging in is drawing a *lot* of power."

Caddie pressed her temples. "I don't like it," she said uneasily. "Mars, I don't like it at all."

Mars didn't like it, either, and just like Caddie, he couldn't say why. Around them, kids were talking, their voices echoing inside the cavernous gym. Mr. Q was standing in the middle of the stage, staring straight at Mars. He kept staring as he walked up to the microphone. Why was he looking at Mars like that?

"All right, all right, H. G. Wells Middle School!" Mr. Q called out, his voice booming across the speakers in the gym. "Are you ready for an assembly or what?"

Everyone cheered, but it was pretty half-hearted. Most of the assemblies were boring.

JP took a sandwich out of their pocket. "I'm hungry. Anybody want some? It's tuna with mayonnaise."

Toothpick liked JP's sandwiches. "Yes, please," he said approvingly.

From Mars's hoodie pocket came a text notification.

"Mars. You're not supposed to have your phone," Caddie whispered.

JP grinned. "Yeah, but who listens to rules? Do you, Cads?"

Mars read the message on his screen out loud.

## Mars · LIL

Thurs, Oct 22, 11:05 am

LIL (Lost in London)
**Friends are not always friends**

"It's LIL!" JP said, smirking, and took a bite of their sandwich. "LOL, Mars! OMG!"

"It sounds like they're giving you advice," Toothpick said. He wiped a splotch of mayonnaise from the corner of his mouth.

"Or a warning," Caddie whispered. "Shush, everyone. Mr. Q is saying something."

*Friends are not always friends.* What did that mean? Mars wondered. And who was LIL?

"... before we kick off this very special event, we need a basketball," Mr. Q was saying to everyone. He cleared his throat. "Mr. Cutty?"

Mr. Cutty, the PE teacher, tossed him a ball.

"What are they doing?" JP wondered. "Free-throw time?"

"All righty!" Mr. Q held up the basketball. "Students, are you ready?"

Students hooted. Someone said, "Start already!"

Caddie clutched Mars's arm, bracing herself.

Mr. Q gave a sweep of his hand at the equipment next to him on the stage. "Through arrangements made by our presenter, we are broadcasting this assembly live around the world!"

"Live around the world?" JP repeated. They swallowed the last of their tuna sandwich.

"Thousands of kids are tuning in right now," Mr. Q said, "to watch this most special presentation."

A hush fell on the gym. Really?

"Is he pulling our leg?" JP asked. "Who would want to watch me eat my tuna sandwich?"

Toothpick pulled on their sleeve. "Not us." He pointed to the stage. "Look."

"Let's give a warm H. G. Wells welcome to our speaker

today," Mr. Q told everyone. He paused and took a dramatic step back. "Oliver Pruitt!"

Mars felt his eyes pop out of his head. Was Mr. Q for real? Then there, walking across the stage, was the man himself. *In their school.* Everyone stood up, clapping wildly.

"Oh my god, it's Oliver Pruitt!" someone yelled behind them.

"Isn't he, like, super rich?" someone else said.

"He's here because of the GIFT," another girl said.

"Can I be in your school, Mr. Pruitt?" someone yelled out.

Meanwhile, Mars was practically having a heart attack. He'd seen so many pictures of Oliver Pruitt. He even had that poster of him in his locker. But none of those pictures had prepared him for what he saw now. Oliver was tall, with dark hair and a goatee, and he wore a tan shirt, a navy blazer, and dark boots. He seemed to shimmer as he walked onstage, as if he was enveloped in a soft, haloed glow. *This* was Oliver Pruitt? This was the man with the laughing voice, who shared hundreds of jokes and riddles on his podcast, who appeared in so many YouTube interviews that it was hard to know if he was real or just something imagined on the Internet? Why did he look so different? And why did he look so familiar, too?

"Namaste!" Oliver Pruitt called out. "Greetings! *Salut! Konnichiwa! Buenos días!*" As he continued greeting the students in languages from all around the world, everyone around Mars was surprised, too. For a moment no one knew what to think. A great murmur went through the crowd.

"Where did he come from?" JP sputtered. "How did he just get up on the stage?"

"He must have been behind the curtains," Toothpick said. "Magicians do that."

"Oliver Pruitt is *not* a magician," Caddie said. Her eyes were not shining in wonder. Instead, she was pressing her head anxiously. "Ugh. My headache is getting worse."

After the crowd subsided, Oliver continued. "Ever since I was little, I have been fascinated by gravity and the speed of light. I wondered: What if we could send messages that way? Because even as a small boy, I knew that a message might be nothing more than an image carried by *the wings of science.*"

Mars trembled in awe. "That's what he was saying on his podcast!" he told his friends.

Oliver now paused to stare meaningfully at the crowd, almost as if he was looking at . . . Mars turned around to see if someone was there behind him. "And to prove my point," Oliver continued, "can I have a volunteer?"

"Me!" shouted someone. Everywhere around them, kids waved their hands, begging to be picked. "Me! Me!"

Oliver looked languidly at them. "Lots of eager students. That's what I like! How about you in the back? Yes, you. Why don't you come down, Mr. Mars Patel?"

His finger was pointed straight at Mars.

"M-m-me?" Mars stammered, surprised. He stood up slowly.

Caddie's hand shot out. "Don't do it," she said immediately.

"Yes, yes, you, Mars." Oliver Pruitt gave a delighted smile.

"How do you know my name?" Mars asked. He was worried, but he was pleased, too. Oliver Pruitt knew who he was? It seemed like a million faces were turned toward Mars, but it was Oliver's face he concentrated on.

Oliver continued smiling easily. "Yes, Mars. I know you," he said pleasantly. "I know all of you. Caddie, JP, Toothpick."

Caddie sucked in her breath.

"Oh my god," JP breathed. "The billionaire guy *does* know who we are."

"And he didn't call me Randall either," Toothpick said approvingly.

"Don't go," Caddie pleaded. "I have a bad feeling, Mars." Her eyes flashed behind her glasses. Mars had never seen her this way—panicky. But Caddie always felt so strongly about everything. Maybe she was getting thrown by Oliver Pruitt being in their gym.

"I have to go," he told her. "Don't worry, Cads. I got it."

Oliver nodded encouragingly. "Good, come, Mars. Come on down to the stage."

"Ask him about Jonas and Aurora," JP urged, their eyes glued to Mars in excitement.

"Mars . . . my head," Caddie warned.

Mars got up, making his way through the crowd.

"Oliver Pruitt knows Mars?" someone said as Mars walked past them down the bleachers.

"Yeah, but he's still a freak," someone else said.

Mars's ears burned, but he kept walking. A hundred questions raced through his mind. He'd dreamed of this moment for so long, the day he'd meet Oliver Pruitt, but he'd never thought it would actually happen. Mars wanted to know how Oliver Pruitt knew him. He wanted to know if he thought they would make it to outer space, if humans would survive all the things that were wrong in this world, and if there was hope for someone like Mars. But most of all, he wanted to know where Aurora and Jonas were, and if Oliver could help find them. Oliver Pruitt could do anything. Could he help Mars and his friends?

Mars reached the bottom of the bleachers. A hush fell across the gym.

"Hi, Mr. Pruitt," he called out nervously. "It's an honor to meet you."

"Yes, come up here to the front. Let's have a good look at you. You're certainly too small to see in the audience."

Everyone laughed.

Mars walked to the stage unsurely. "Like here?" he asked.

"Closer. Closer. Yes, don't be shy. Mr. Q, give him the ball."

The ball?

Mr. Q walked to Mars, basketball in hand. His face was closely shaved and pale, and there were dark circles under his eyes. "Here you go, Mars," he said. Then he whispered, "Good luck."

In the bleachers, Mars could see that his friends had come down to the front row. They were watching curiously—at least, JP and Toothpick were. Caddie looked positively ill.

"OK, I have the ball," Mars said. He took a deep breath. "And a few questions, too." That was good. He was calm. He could do this. Talk to his hero *and* get his questions answered.

Oliver Pruitt held out his hands. "First things first. I want you to throw the ball at me, Mars. Throw it hard! Right at me."

"Throw the ball?" Mars asked, confused. He looked at the basketball in his hands as if he were seeing it for the first time.

"That's right, Mars. They do teach you how to throw a basketball in this school, don't they?"

Everyone laughed loudly again.

"Throw the ball, Patel!" Kids started yelling.

"Throw the ball, Martian!"

That last one was Clyde Boofsky's voice. Mars knew even without looking.

Fine. They wanted him to throw the ball? He could do that.

Mars heaved the ball with force at Oliver Pruitt's outstretched hands, and everyone saw it at the same time: the basketball went sailing right through Oliver's hands, right through his entire body, then bounced against the curtains behind him.

Everyone gasped. Oliver Pruitt wasn't there!

"He's not onstage!" Mars shouted, astonished. "That's not him!"

Oliver tipped his head back and laughed.

"That's right, Mars. As you can all see, I'm not here." Oliver held his arms out and turned around, and this time Mars noticed his boots were silent against the floor. "I'm somewhere else. But what you observe now is my image. I'm a hologram! Think of that! I'm a message, a beam of light, traveling on the wings of science!"

The place was in an uproar. Oliver Pruitt wasn't real! Oliver Pruitt was a genius! Oliver Pruitt was going to rule the world with his inventions! What was going to happen next?

Mars was still standing on the stage. He didn't know what to think. Why would Oliver Pruitt do this, be on a stage, broadcast to millions of kids around the world, while trying to fool everyone? Was this just some kind of game? Or was that the point? Mars thought hard, then he suddenly had an idea. That's it!

"Mr. Pruitt, if you're a hologram," Mars said breathlessly, "is Pruitt Prep a hologram, too?"

For the first time, Oliver stopped smiling. The sun went out behind his eyes. "I think you need to improve your basketball skills, Mars," he said.

By now the kids in the bleachers had settled down, but when they heard him say that, they all started to laugh.

"Let someone else throw the ball," someone called out.

"Yeah, Martian Patel can't throw."

"He sucks!"

Mars ignored the voices behind him.

"But you didn't answer my question," Mars said. "Is Pruitt Prep real, or is it a beam of light?"

Isn't that what his podcast was about? A beam of light? Maybe the school was a trick, too. Not real. Even if that didn't completely make sense either.

"I never said this was a Q-and-A session, Mr. Patel," Oliver said shortly. "It's time for you to sit back down."

Something had changed in Oliver Pruitt's face. All of a sudden, he didn't look so smug. Why wouldn't he answer the question?

"My friends are missing," Mars continued. "Do you know where they are?"

Mr. Q stepped forward. "Careful, Mars," he warned.

There was no mistaking it now. Oliver Pruitt was scowling at Mars!

Mars wavered. Had he done something wrong? Should he stop? This was Oliver Pruitt, the person he'd wanted to be all his life. He'd listened to every podcast ever aired. He'd emailed the answer to every riddle. Oliver seemed upset that Mars was asking him questions, but what if he had the answer Mars was looking for? Mars pressed on. "Are Aurora and Jonas at your school? Are they at Pruitt Prep?"

"Mr. Patel," Fagan called out, suddenly appearing on the stage. "Please step down at once!"

Meanwhile Oliver shot a look at Fagan and Mr. Q. "Is *this* what you encourage at this school? Crazy conspiracy theories?"

"We're deeply sorry, Mr. Pruitt," Fagan said. "Mars has always been a discipline problem."

"That's why we give him detention, sir," said Mr. Q.

"Well, it's obviously not working!" Oliver said snidely. "You disappoint me, Mars. I would expect a *lot* more from you."

His words stung. Where was the Oliver Pruitt who made

jokes and told riddles, and even seemed to be giving Mars clues on his podcast? Wasn't he the one who'd warned Mars about the Code Red, and about heading to the clearing when they were on the island? It had always felt like Oliver Pruitt was secretly on his side.

This man wasn't on Mars's side. This man sounded like a jerk.

"Answer my question, Mr. Pruitt," Mars shouted. "And I don't *care* if you're a hologram!"

Oliver narrowed his eyes. It was amazing how lifelike he was, down to his eyebrows and shock of hair. "Mars . . . you said you were surprised that I know you. But I've known you for years. All those letters I received from you: 'Dear Mr. Pruitt, You're my idol. I want to be just like you!'" His voice turned singsongy and mean.

Mars felt tears spring to his eyes. "I—did," he said hoarsely.

"By the time I was your age, I'd designed my first fully automated car. What have you done with your life, Mars?" Oliver demanded. "Angered your teachers? Pranked your school? You think *that's* progress? Running around with your clueless friends? What else have you done?"

"I—I don't know," Mars whispered. A feeling of awfulness swelled in him. From the bleachers Mars's friends watched in horror. JP looked seriously pissed.

"Instead of accusing me," Oliver said, "you should ask,

why did Aurora and Jonas disappear in the first place? Is it *your* fault for leading them in the wrong direction? Are you the one who's a bad leader?"

"He's not!" JP's voice shot angrily across the gym.

"Quiet, Ms. McGowan!" Fagan scolded.

Oliver wasn't finished. "Maybe it's time to admit that *you're* the failure, Mars Patel."

Everything he said felt like an arrow striking Mars down.

"Why are you doing this?" Mars cried. "You were my hero, and now . . ." His voice cracked.

"Loser!" someone called from the bleachers.

"Mars is a loser!"

"Get him off the stage!"

"Loser! Loser! Loser!" It became a deafening chant inside the gym.

Oliver the hologram remained onstage. He was so real-looking, but now Mars knew he was a fake. "Hmm, Mars, are those tears I see?" he asked with exaggerated concern. "If you can't take the heat, then get out of the kitchen. Go sit down!"

"Sit down, Mars! Sit down, Mars!" echoed the crowd.

"You know what? I'm going to find them!" Mars shouted.

"Sit down, Mars! Sit down, Mars!"

Mars backed away. White anger flashed through him. Oliver Pruitt wasn't going to get away with this. Not now. Not after this.

Oliver watched from the stage, and it seemed like he was growing bigger and bigger with every second. "And what if you fail, Mars?" His voice boomed across the gym while everyone was yelling at the same time. "What are you going to do now when so far you've done NOTHING? I see—go ahead, then, run away like you always do, and—"

Mars had reached the gym doors as Oliver called out after him, when there was a loud squall and the sound cut instantly.

"JP McGowan!" Fagan's furious voice rose above the din.

Through the crowd Mars saw JP standing at the front of the stage, grinning and defiant. In their hand, they held a cable. JP had unplugged the entire sound system.

"That's how I roll, people!" JP yelled.

# 14
## POKING THE TIGER

In the hall, waves of anger pulsed through Mars. Inside the gym he'd felt pounded on all sides, by the kids in the bleachers, by Mr. Q standing there doing nothing, by Fagan playing kiss-up, but most of all by Oliver Pruitt, who seemed to know every sad thought Mars had ever had, and had broadcast it to the entire world.

But what Oliver Pruitt didn't know was that the same anger that had turned Mars speechless in the gym made him spring into action in the hall. By the time he reached his locker, Mars knew *exactly* what to do.

"Mars!"

He looked up to see Caddie, JP, and Toothpick running up to him.

"We were looking for you! And Fagan is looking for you, too!" Caddie said.

"Well, she found *me*!" JP said. "One week of detention for unplugging Oliver Pruitt!"

"One week of detention is nothing for you," Toothpick observed proudly. "You could do that in your sleep."

"Maybe I will!" JP said, grinning.

"What are you doing, Mars?" Caddie asked.

"Texting Aurora," JP guessed.

"No." Mars handed his phone to Caddie. "Just setting my phone up. Since you're here, you can take the video of me."

She looked at him, doubtful. "What's it about?"

"Start recording," he told her.

Caddie cleared her throat. "OK, here we go. Three, two, one, now."

Mars took a deep breath and began. "Oliver Pruitt, you have our friends, Aurora and Jonas. And when you mess with a friend of Mars Patel, you don't just get me, you get all of us. You think you have the whole world fooled. But you don't fool me anymore. You're a liar and a bully and I know you're hiding something. We will find out what it is. And we will RUIN you. I don't care how rich and how smart you are. You are going down! Mars out."

"Cut," Caddie said.

"That's awesome!" JP cried.

"OK, hit send," Mars said.

"Where are you sending it, Mars?" Caddie asked.

"Oliver Pruitt's website," he said. "Social media, You-Tube, the works."

"No one's ever sent something like that to Oliver Pruitt," Toothpick said. "It will go viral."

"But Mars," Caddie said, "if I hit this send button . . ."

Before she could finish, JP leaned across and pressed the green button on the phone.

"Mission accomplished," JP said. "I think."

Caddie stared incredulously at everyone. "Oh my god, guys, do you know what this means? Mars just declared war on the most powerful man on this planet!"

"No, Caddie," JP said. "WE did."

**From: dfagan@hgwellsmiddeschool.org**
**To: H. G. Wells Middle School Parents**
**Date: Thursday, October 22, 3:00 p.m.**
**Subject: GIFT Test is TOMORROW**

Dear Parents,

This is a reminder that the GIFT test is TOMORROW. *Anyone who misses the GIFT risks academic probation. Students already on probation who miss the test can face suspension and even expulsion.* More information on the GIFT can be found at www.pruittprep.edu, including school founder Oliver Pruitt's intriguing essay: "Make Way for the Smart Kids!" Please have your child report to homeroom tomorrow morning. *Be on time!* And remember our motto: "Every Success for Every Child." Success means PUNCTUALITY.

Sincerely,

Dorena Fagan

Principal

H. G. Wells Middle School

## Ma · Mars

Ma

Mars! Are you up?

GIFT is today.

Why not answering your phone?

You better be getting ready for school

you know I can't call you again until lunch

You're not listening to that podcast are you?

# FROM THE PODCAST

Listeners, you know what they say about tigers:

they're majestic, beautiful, instinctive.

But what happens when you poke the tiger?

When something so powerful feels threatened, there's

NO TELLING WHAT HE WILL DO.

To the stars!

1320 Comments

thisismars    8 hours ago
OP we're onto u and ur going down

allie_j    7 hours ago
ur the kid in the assembly right

galaxygenius    1 hour ago
Is OP the tiger or is mars

oreocookies    42 min ago
is OP real or a hologram

lostinlondon    38 min ago
he's real

## Mars · Caddie · JP · Toothpick

Mars
**guyz did u hear OP**

JP
**sry I have better things to do**

Toothpick
**I did mars is in trouble**

Caddie
**Omg wut did he say**

Mars
**he wants to eat me alive**

JP
**he doesn't know who he's messing with**

Toothpick
**GIFT starts after homeroom**

Caddie
**Here at school already**

**mom freaked about me being late**

JP
**B there in 5**

Toothpick
**B there in 2.5**

Mars
**B there I don't know when**

Caddie
**Hurry mars**

Mars
**meet me on the front lawn guys**

Mars
**hey wuts that buzzing sound**

# 15

## VIRAL

**W**hy doesn't Oliver Pruitt say these things to your face, Mars?" JP asked. "Why does he have to threaten you on his podcast? Maybe he's scared we're going to kick his butt."

They were standing on the front lawn before the first bell rang. In a few minutes the GIFT test would be starting.

"I don't know," Caddie said doubtfully. "He is the world's most powerful man, JP."

"Why do you keep looking at the sky, Mars?" asked Toothpick. "There isn't rain in the forecast until noon. Just clouds and fog now. I checked this morning."

"Does anyone else hear that buzzing sound?" Mars said. "I feel like it's been following me or something."

"You think it's Oliver Pruitt sending a saber-toothed tiger after you?" JP said.

Mars shrugged. "I don't think he meant a real tiger, JP. He was being *metaphorical.*"

"Or diabolical," Toothpick said. "Because he's Oliver Pruitt."

"When did Oliver go from being a good guy," Caddie wondered, "to being a bad guy?"

"Like, yesterday," JP said. "Remember the assembly? We don't need a HOLOGRAM throwing shade. Who cares if he's got rocket ships? I don't even want to take the GIFT anymore."

"It's mandatory," Toothpick said. "Anyone who misses it faces probation. Or worse."

"Yeah, yeah," JP said. "Tell me something I don't know."

"JP's right," Mars said. "Why should I take the GIFT either? I don't want to go Pruitt Prep. Not after what Oliver Pruitt did in the gym." And not if Oliver was out to get him.

"If he's out to get you," Caddie said, "then he's out to get all of us."

"Doing it again," Mars said. "Being there in my head."

"Sorry," she said, sighing. "I guess I'm tired. My mom made me stay up last night doing flash cards. She thinks the GIFT is my last chance to straighten up or I'm a failure for life."

"How could anyone say that about you?" JP said. "You're perfect."

"That's not what my mom says," Caddie said.

"Why does the school even care what Oliver Pruitt thinks?" Mars asked.

"Well, everyone cares what *you* think of Oliver Pruitt, Mars," Toothpick said. He had been looking at his phone. "Your video message to him has been viewed 1.3 million times."

"Dude, you're famous!" JP exclaimed.

"That's probably why he wants to kill me," Mars said.

"I'm sure Oliver Pruitt doesn't want to kill you," Caddie said. She stopped.

They all looked up. This time they all heard it.

"See? It's that buzzing sound," Mars said. "What *is* that?"

Toothpick pushed up his glasses and studied the sky. "It's a drone," he said matter-of-factly.

JP narrowed their eyes. "Say what?"

"You mean, like, a flying robot?" Mars asked incredulously.

They all looked at a gray, metallic object that was now moving in rapid circles over their heads.

"It looks like a gigantic mosquito," JP said.

"A drone is a small unmanned aircraft," Toothpick explained. "The military uses them for surveillance, target spotting, reconnaissance, and weaponry."

"Weaponry? You mean like braining people?" JP picked up their backpack from the ground. "OK, maybe it's time to take the GIFT—inside!"

"Look out!" Mars yelled. "It's coming right at us!"

Caddie lunged to the right and JP lunged to the left, which left Mars to duck straight down. Meanwhile, Toothpick remained standing, watching the whole thing curiously.

There was a loud crash a few feet in front of him.

"What the heck?" JP said, jumping up.

Toothpick bent down over the metal object that had veered into a nearby boulder. Now that it was on the ground, they could all see it was small enough to fit inside the palm of a hand. Toothpick poked it with a pencil. "Well, now it's a broken drone."

"Attention, all students!" came an announcement over the PA. "Please report to your homerooms immediately. GIFT testing will be starting shortly."

Mars was leaning over next to Toothpick. "Is that a Pruitt logo on the side?" he asked cautiously.

Toothpick nodded. "Let's say Oliver Pruitt knows where you are. Or at least he wants to." He picked up the broken drone and put it in his backpack. "I'm going to take a closer look at it. Knowing Oliver, this won't be the last drone following you."

"More drones?" Mars asked.

"Oliver wouldn't just send one and let it crash," Toothpick said. "Maybe this was a warning drone."

"Great," Mars said. "Just what I needed."

"Come on, guys," Caddie said. "We'd better go in. Let's not be late to the GIFT."

🎧

**Inside the school, JP took out a ham sandwich and chewed** it quickly on the way to homeroom. JP could still feel their heart pounding, remembering the drone. It was one thing to say you would do something; it was another thing to well . . . *do* something. Was Oliver Pruitt actually after them with his saber-toothed drone?

Homeroom didn't help JP's nerves.

"Out of my way, They-Them," Clyde Boofsky said, smirking.

"Or can we just call her It?" wondered his evil minion pal, Scott Bane.

"Even my dog knows she's a she," Clyde said. "I guess she's smarter than you, JP."

JP gave them both a one-two shove. Then all was cool. But man, JP was getting tired of this stuff. JP sat down, eating the last of their ham sandwich gloomily. Why couldn't life be more like a sandwich?

JP loved making their own lunches, and the way they got to choose how to make a sandwich, with layers of meat and cheese and lettuce dabbed in ranch dressing. Sometimes JP made a killer chili with red beans that they brought in their thermos, and it was spiced up so it gave a nice burn down your throat. Their food was like a perfect universe of flavors and textures and happiness.

Toothpick liked JP's sandwiches, too. In fourth grade, JP had noticed how the others would pick on Toothpick all the time. He never did anything to stop them, even when they stole his backpack or tied his shoes together under the desk. So JP started following him around. At first, Toothpick didn't like it. "But you're not street smart," JP told him. "That's why I'm here."

"I know the direction of home," he said. "And I have a good sense of due north."

JP smacked their forehead. "That's just it. You don't know the real rules of the game, like what people say and do right before they're about to pound into you."

He thought for a moment. "You mean the bullying?"

"You need someone to show you the ropes," JP said.

"That would be you?"

JP grinned. "I don't even charge. All I ask is that you and I eat lunch together every day. I keep the creeps away from you, and you . . ." They paused. "You try my sandwiches and tell me how they are. And you talk to me. You're more interesting than these turkeys here."

Soon JP began bringing Toothpick lunches, too. They were tasty, full of carbs and proteins and unusual flavors (his favorite was the chili). In return, Toothpick talked about quantum physics and JP would say, "That's cool," even without understanding what he was saying all the time. That's how their friendship grew. Like, Toothpick could tell when JP was in a bad mood because of something that happened in homeroom, and then he'd talk about soccer. He'd share league stats he'd looked up on his phone, which he probably didn't have a clue about, but it always made JP feel better. Not because they were talking soccer, but because Toothpick cared. He cared deeply about many things; he just wasn't good at showing it.

That's probably what made Epica so annoying. Lately, whenever Epica was around, Pick lit up like a firefly. Suddenly Pick was showing feelings, but for someone who wasn't JP. And JP hated that.

Boofsky and Bane were watching from the back row, making disgusting kissy faces. JP gave them the death glare with a finger across the neck in a slicing motion. That got the two of them to shut up, but for how long? Soon they'd be onto some other poor kid in class. It never ended.

Maybe JP did need to take this GIFT after all. Get the heck out of this school. But where would the GIFT land someone except at Pruitt Prep? Was Oliver Pruitt a crazed genius or a crazed criminal? Or just plain crazy?

# 16
# THE GIFT

**M**ars, Caddie, and Toothpick had homeroom together. As soon as Toothpick sat down, he looked at the clock to see how many minutes he had before the GIFT started. Not much time to look up drone operating systems . . .

"Hi, Randall!" Toothpick didn't even have to look up to know who it was.

Epica was sitting one desk down, with two pencils sharpened and ready to go in front of her.

"Hi, Epica," Toothpick said right away. "Ready for the GIFT?"

"I'm always ready for school." She was wearing a crisp blue blazer with the school's emblem on the front pocket. No one knew where she got these blazers since there wasn't actually a school uniform. "That's the advantage of being you and me. We're always ready."

"Um, yeah," Toothpick said.

"I mean, did you even study?" Epica asked. "You're already so smart."

"Sorta," Toothpick said. The GIFT was one of those exams with little information circulating on the Internet. No one knew what would be on it because the exam changed every year. Toothpick hadn't been sure how to study for it, but he figured that a review of the periodic table, Homer's *The Odyssey*, and Latin conjugates would be enough. As a precaution, he'd also memorized the back of three cereal boxes this morning in case there were any questions on popular culture or breakfast.

"After the GIFT is done, maybe you and I can—" Epica was interrupted by the sound of Mr. Q entering the room. He was carrying his usual neon-green clipboard.

"You and I can . . . ?" Toothpick prompted Epica. But she had fallen silent as Mr. Q spoke. So Toothpick tried to think of how that sentence might end. *You and I can go to the beach to plot the coordinates of the next gale storm to reach Port Elizabeth.* Or more simple: *you and I can go to the beach.* That would be awesome. The Port Elizabeth beach was rocky and full of crab shells and sand dollars. Was Epica the kind of girl to collect sand dollars and bleach them until they were pearly white? Toothpick had three of them on his desk at home. They were the most beautiful things he owned.

"All right, put your phones away," Mr. Q said, "and all other handheld devices. You will not be able to take them with you to the library, where the test is administered."

Toothpick considered the broken drone in his backpack. Did that count as a device? Maybe not, since he wasn't technically holding it in his hand, and also because it was currently dead.

"Did you see Mr. Q?" Mars whispered from behind Toothpick. "He's looking at us funny."

"You still think we can't trust Mr. Q?" Caddie whispered back.

Just then Mars's phone pinged.

"Mars," Caddie whispered insistently. "You *have* to put your phone away. Mr. Q said."

"Hey, guys," Mars said, surprised, "I just a got a voice message from LIL."

"LIL?" Toothpick asked. "You mean Lost in London?"

"Mr. Mars," Mr. Q called from the front. "I can see your phone. I'm giving you until I finish taking attendance to put that phone away. That goes for all of you. Two minutes to power down."

"Listen to this," Mars whispered. He played the voice mail quietly.

*"Mars, this is Julia, aka Lost in London. I watched your video and it was awesome! You're great, Mars,*

*and I can tell you that what you said is going to make a huge difference. But now you're needed elsewhere. Don't take the GIFT test. Go to the Luckstone Warehouse. Now. You'll find what you're looking for."*

"'What you're looking for'?" Caddie repeated. "Why is she asking you to go to Luckstone? That place has been abandoned for years. She's insane."

"Look," Mars's breath exploded. "What if Julia's right? What if she knows what I'm looking for? I have to go. And I have to go now."

"Mars Patel! Caddie Patchett!" Mr. Q barked from the front. "Cell phones off. Everyone, please get packed up. We are lining up in exactly one minute to go the library."

"Mars, stop," Caddie pleaded. "You think you're going to find Aurora and Jonas there. But what if you don't? How do you know you can trust this Julia? Besides, Mr. Q will see you leaving."

Mars turned to Toothpick. "What do you think?"

"Missing the GIFT could ruin your life," Toothpick said.

"Thanks, Pick," Mars said.

"Unless," he mused, "there's a natural disaster, an act of God, or some other disruption to cause a delay." Toothpick tried to think of anything else that could preempt the GIFT. Getting an emergency root canal?

Mars sighed. "Well, maybe that's what we need—a

disaster. Something has to change, or who knows—one of us is going to disappear next."

"Excuse me," Caddie said suddenly. And she was gone.

"Wait, I didn't mean literally," Mars said. "Where did she go?"

"Bathroom?" Toothpick guessed.

"Really? Like, right before the GIFT? But she didn't even help me—" Mars stopped.

"Decide what to do next?" Toothpick asked. "You rely on Caddie a lot, don't you?"

"No, I don't!" Mars said. "I mean . . . OK, maybe I do."

Just then the PA came on. "Attention, attention, students. A pack of wild wolves has entered the front door of the school. They are in the halls and extremely deadly. Seek cover immediately!"

Chaos erupted in the room. Everyone was immediately up from their chairs, talking and yelling at the same time.

Mars was dumbstruck. "It's Caddie. That's Caddie, isn't it?"

"Also, please note," she added over the PA, "the GIFT has been delayed by ONE HOUR."

Toothpick looked at Mars over the din. "I believe that's your cue," he said.

Mars grinned. As students hysterically debated the size and number of wild wolves inside the school, and whether they were all going to die, he disappeared. In the front, Mr.

Q said something under his breath that might or might not have been inappropriate for students to hear.

"This is a disaster," Epica said, glaring.

"At least it isn't a flood," Toothpick said. "Floods and droughts kill more people than other natural disasters." He hoped that would make Epica feel better. She looked genuinely upset. She must really want to take the GIFT. Maybe if she knew this delay was for the greater good, it would help, but Toothpick had to keep quiet for the sake of his friends. So instead he gave her a stick of his favorite gum, Hubba Bubba, and she smiled at last.

At the front, Mr. Q still looked like he didn't know what to do. He was eyeing the mayhem going on around him and seemed to accept the fact that within a few minutes, the school had become crazy town. Meanwhile, Toothpick reached into his backpack.

"Whatcha got there?" Epica asked, blowing a bubble.

Toothpick leaned his backpack over so she could see better.

Her eyes widened. "Is that what I think it is?"

"And I have an idea what to do with it," he said.

**From:** dfagan@hgwellsmiddeschool.org
**To:** staff@hgwellsmiddleschool.org
**Date:** Friday, October 23, 9:12 a.m.
**Subject:** GIFT is ON

Dear FACULTY AND STAFF,

Please disregard prior announcement concerning wolves. Port Elizabeth has not had a wolf problem since the autumn of 1983. Out of an abundance of caution, we will administer the GIFT starting fourth period after lunch—ON THE HOUR.

Sincerely,
Dorena Fagan
Principal
H. G. Wells Middle School

## Wolf Outbreak in Port Elizabeth?

**Port Elizabeth, WA—**There has been an unconfirmed report this morning of a wolf outbreak in the vicinity of H. G. Wells Middle School.

"I heard them growling outside the window," said one student, Bianca Elderberry.

"We don't know what to do," said another student, Max Blink. "Like, is this another Code Red?"

Students were about to take the nationally administered GIFT test.

"Everything is under control," said Principal Dorena Fagan, who still plans to administer the test in the afternoon. "Nothing stops the GIFT."

Some students are taking the change in stride.

"I'm ready for the GIFT no matter what," said honor student Epica Hernandez.

Every year, students around the country and the world take the GIFT test, which is used by schools and colleges for assessment purposes. It also serves as a prerequisite for entrance to the prestigious Pruitt Prep Academy on nearby Gale Island. Acceptance rates are stringently low, and students must show other signs of extraordinary academic merit to get in. For students like Epica Hernandez, entry to the school is a must.

"A few wolves aren't going to stop me," she said. ∎

## Saira Patel's Voice Mail

"Ma, it's me, Mars. Sorry my voice is muffled. It's hard to talk when you're biking in the rain. Anyway, you're going to get a phone call from school. You're not going to be happy. I'm sorry to disappoint you, but I'm doing this for my friends. . . . Most people try to knock you down even before you get anywhere. Not my friends. They always hold me up. If you came to my school, you'd see that. You'd get why I'm on my bike in the rain.

"Oh yeah, one other thing. There's a drone following me. It's the second one I've seen today, and it might be trying to kill me. So if I don't call again, maybe you should find out about the drone. Mars, out."

# 17

# THE WAREHOUSE

Mars didn't realize how creepy an abandoned ware-house could be. First, no electricity. As he entered, he was greeted with pitch-darkness. Second, there was a dripping noise as he felt a giant splat of water fall on his cheek. And *then* something scurried across his feet.

"Ack!" he shouted. Was it a mouse? A rat? His scream echoed through the cavernous room, sending a flock of winged creatures (bats?) into the rafters. Great. He wasn't alone after all. He had the whole animal kingdom with him.

At least he had lost the drone. He had been surprised to see another hovering over him as he left the school on his bike. But then he remembered what Pick had said—there would be more drones. Pick had been right. As usual.

This one had followed him relentlessly down the old highway, dipping dangerously close so that he could hear it whirring right behind his ears. It was so terrifying that he'd swerved right in front of a truck, and for a moment, Mars had seen his life flash before his eyes. Then he'd made it to the other side of the road. The truck honked loudly as Mars slipped away in the other direction and finally ditched the drone.

*Oliver's trying to kill me,* Mars thought. One way or another.

"Jonas?" Mars called out now into the dark warehouse. "Aurora?"

There was a loud crackle on the ground.

"Who's there?" Mars said quickly. "Oliver Pruitt?" His feet kicked something metallic. He stooped and picked it up. "You better stop. I have this crowbar in my hand." He wasn't sure what a crowbar was, but he figured it sounded dangerous. "And I'm not afraid to use it!"

"Mars?" said a familiar voice.

"Caddie?" Mars was dumbstruck.

"Surprise," she said.

"What are you doing here? You *followed* me?"

She gave a small smile. "Yeah. You're OK, right?"

"Yeah, but . . . Caddie, what about the GIFT? You were worried about being late. Now you won't even . . ."

"Let my mom worry about the GIFT now. Oof," she stumbled forward as he met her halfway and stepped on her foot. "Ouch!"

"Sorry, Caddie!" he said. He reached to steady both of

them in the dark. "I guess we'll be great at the dance, huh? Since I'm good at stepping on your feet."

Caddie smiled some more. "Yeah. And I'll probably step on yours."

"We are still going to the dance tonight, aren't we?" Things had been strange ever since they'd gone to Gale Island. But did Caddie feel the same way?

"I can't believe it's tonight already," Caddie said. "So much is going on. But, yes. I'd love that. I mean, as long as we're not expelled."

Behind them came a creaking sound, and suddenly a door opened as outside light filtered in.

"JP! Toothpick! Wait, you're *all* here?"

"Oh, yeah," Caddie said. "They came, too."

"Of course. What did you expect?" JP said. "Who wants to take that stupid GIFT anyway?"

"Actually, I can think of one person," Toothpick said.

"I'm not talking about Epica Hernandez," JP said. "And boy, this place is a mess! Ick, look—puddles everywhere. Is that LIL person around? I don't see anybody here but us."

"JP thinks LIL's message was a hoax," Toothpick said. "But I disagree. Whoever it is did their homework. They warned you about the assembly. And look what happened with Oliver Pruitt." He looked around curiously. "Do you hear that?"

"You mean the drips?" JP asked.

"Shush," Mars said. Everyone stopped talking. "I don't believe it," he said.

A buzzing sound came in the distance, and got louder and louder.

"Oh no—JP opened the door and let the drone in!" Mars exclaimed.

"What, didn't it die at H. G.?" JP cried, crouching low.

"It's another one," Mars said, his hands raised protectively over his head.

"Then run for your life!" JP wailed.

"No, wait." Toothpick pointed to the dark gray unit that circled overhead. "This one is carrying something." Around and around it traveled, coming closer until, with one careful move, it deposited a brown paper package squarely on the ground. Then it flew out the same way it had come.

"I don't believe it," Mars said again.

"You keep repeating yourself," Toothpick said, "when it's obvious that we're all seeing the same thing."

"Maybe the package is booby-trapped," JP said. "Nobody open it."

Caddie furrowed her brow. "I think it's safe. I'm not getting any bad vibes."

"I'll open it." Toothpick moved forward quickly. "This is a mystery that can be solved."

"Yeah, but will you live to tell about it?" JP muttered.

The package was covered in ordinary brown paper, with

colored string wrapped several times around. The shape was long and narrow, and there were no markings on it. Toothpick used his house key to cut through the knots. Then he ripped the package open.

"It's papers," he announced. He pulled them out. "Hundreds of papers."

Everyone crowded around him.

"They're flyers," Caddie said, "of missing children! Look at that."

"This one is Lily from Perth, Australia," Caddie said. *"Have you seen Lily?"*

"This is Herman from Guatemala," Mars said.

"This is written in Chinese," JP said.

"Here's one from Julia in London," Mars said, holding the flyer up. "Lost in London."

"Look, it's Jonas!" Caddie held up a flyer with a photo of Jonas wearing his Mariners baseball cap.

"And here's Aurora!" JP said.

Mars leaned forward. "I took that picture on her phone," he exclaimed.

There was Aurora, holding a Sharpie in her hand. She had struck a bold pose next to the words she'd scrawled on the school's back wall: MOPS 4-EVER. It had been a rare sunny day, and she was squinting a little. Mars remembered angling the phone so he got both her and the graffiti tag inside the photo. Was that only a few weeks ago? It felt like forever. Just seeing the photo now sent a shiver down his back.

Everyone had fallen silent, seeing the flyers with their friends' faces on them.

"Why would LIL want us to see these flyers?" JP finally asked. "And use a drone to send them . . . here?" Above them, rainwater continued to drip from the rafters, leaving puddles across the dilapidated floor.

"Drones can be used from far away," Toothpick said. "She can't get to us, so this is the next best thing."

"Buy why use Oliver Pruitt's drone?" JP asked.

Mars jumped up. "Because it's a clue. Don't you see? Kids are missing all over the world, not just Aurora and Jonas. And maybe what Julia is trying to tell us is that *Oliver Pruitt is behind it!*"

## 18
# WORTH FIGHTING FOR

**W**hen Mars returned to his apartment later that afternoon, he was greeted by big boxes. For the first time he could remember, his mother was home early. And she was packing.

"M-m-ma," he stammered, surprised. "What's going on? Why are you packing?"

Saira Patel stopped to look at him. She was still dressed in a dark turtleneck and leggings, and her hair was up in her customary ponytail. But now there were dark lines around her eyes where her eyeliner had run. She had been crying. Mars had never seen his mother cry in his life.

"So, Mars," she said, her voice steely. "How was the GIFT?"

Mars's stomach dropped. "You got my voice mail, right? Did the school call you?"

"The school did," she continued, her voice as icy as

before. "Principal Fagan called me, as a matter of fact. You know why? To tell me that you are EXPELLED!"

"Expelled?" Mars said, gulping. He knew that would be a possibility, but he'd never really expected the school to go through with it. "But that's wack! Who cares if I take the GIFT or not?"

"Don't you get it? We are finished here. This community—it's over!"

Mars looked fearfully at her. "What do you mean? We can go and talk to Fagan, right? She's just trying to scare us!"

Saira shook her head. "Enough. We are moving to Cleveland. Tomorrow. I knew all along. This place is no good for you. You have bad influences in school. Too many mistakes. I thought it would be all right living here. Close to . . . well, I see now. I was wrong. We need a fresh start. We need to get away from the bad influences. ALL of them."

"My friends aren't bad influences, Mamaji," Mars cried. "They're good. I'm sure I can convince Fagan to let me back in. I can't leave now. Aurora and Jonas aren't the only missing kids."

"We aren't discussing this, Mars, beta," she said firmly. "My decision is final. Tomorrow. I will be done packing soon. I've made all the arrangements."

Mars staggered back. All along, his mother had been warning him about moving to Cleveland. But he'd never taken her seriously. He walked slowly to his room and was stunned to find everything gone. His clothes, his books, even his computer and charging cords. On his bed lay the toy rocket. For some reason, Saira had not packed it yet. He picked it up, feeling the familiar fabric under his fingers.

He needed more time. He couldn't leave tomorrow when there was so much left to do and he was in touch with Lost in London about the missing children. He was so close to solving the mystery. He'd seen the flyers, he'd seen the pictures of his friends, and now it wasn't just about them—Oliver Pruitt could be involved, too. One way or another, Mars had to get to the bottom of it. If only there was a way to hold his mom off.

And Caddie! Tonight was the dance. He had promised her. Mars's mind raced. He still had his backpack, his coat, and his phone. And his bike.

Mars put the toy rocket back on the bed and went to the living room, where his mom was wrapping up framed photos. The last items left on the mantel of a fireplace that hadn't seen a single fire. Saira never had time to make one.

"Ma . . ." he started softly.

Saira was lost in thought, looking at a photo of her with Mars as a toddler, wearing a bright-red knitted hat. It was her and him. It had always been her and him as long as Mars could remember.

He swallowed. "Ma . . . you worked so hard. Like, this must have taken you all day."

Saira turned to him. "Yes, Manu," she said. Her voice was throaty. "I guess we didn't have much to begin with. But we have each other, right?" She smiled tightly. "A fresh new start, that's what we need."

"So . . . let me get takeout, OK? Like, one more time Pepe's Pizza, OK? I don't think Cleveland has pizza like they make, right?"

Saira shook her head. "I'm not hungry. We still have some bread and jam in the fridge."

"No, I'll run out and get it, OK, Ma? I won't be long. They're just around the corner."

Saira studied him for a moment. "Be back in fifteen minutes. I mean it. You better not disappoint me."

"Of course," Mars said easily. "I always come home, right? See you in the stars!"

Saira smiled unconsciously at their old saying.

"*Chalo, chalte hai.* Come quickly, Mars. Don't delay," she said. "I'll see you in the stars."

Mars gathered his coat and ran outside to where he had left his bike leaning against the apartment building. His heart was heavy. He'd never thought this day would come. His mother was silent, mysterious, going some-where each day without telling him where. There were too many secrets, too much sadness, and in her eyes flashed a hidden anger, not at him but at something Mars didn't understand. Even so, he loved her. She was his Ma. There was no one else in his life who had always been there. Except for his friends.

And now they needed him. They were worth fighting for, especially when he had lost everything else. "Here I go," he whispered to himself, kicking off with his bike. "Forgive me, Ma."

He pedaled rapidly down Chinook Street. He knew which way to go. And he didn't need to look behind to know the drone was following him.

# FROM THE PODCAST

15 ▶ 30

Listeners, do you know about drones?

They're very good at reaching places people can't.

They're good for other things, too.

Hunting, finding, destroying.

It's no surprise that I own an ARMY OF DRONES.

Does that make me smart or dangerous?

To the stars!

**5100 Comments** ⊗

galaxygenius   40 min ago
I don't get it is this another one of ur riddles

allie_j   30 min ago
OP is smart we know that

galaxygenius   28 min ago
yeah but this sounds like a threat

oreocookies   19 min ago
I think it has something to do with that guy mars

lostinlondon    8 min ago
mars is closer than he thinks

allie_j    2 min ago
can I still get into Pruitt Prep if I don't know the answer to
ur drone qtn

## 19

# DANCE BREAK

**H. G. WELLS DANCE PARTY!!**
Come for sick jams & dance the night away!!!
Friday, Oct. 23, 7–9 p.m.
H. G. Wells Middle School Gym
**DJ • PHOTO BOOTH • GIVEAWAYS • PIZZA**

**Security and surveillance at all times**
**Don't worry, parents—we've got your kids covered!**

🎧

It was dark by the time Mars reached Caddie's old tree house. It had been years since anyone had been up inside it. Caddie's father had told her it was condemned, and that he ought to take it down before it crashed to the ground. Despite that, the tree house had remained, and its sorry state didn't deter Mars. He crawled up the ladder inside the tree house, pushing aside a weather-beaten board game that had become unrecognizable from mildew and dust.

The tree house was cold and dark, but it was dry. Maybe he could hide out here forever. He didn't need much, just granola bars and water and maybe potato chips. It wasn't like he could go back to his place, not with his mom's plan to move to Cleveland.

A zip line connected the tree house to Caddie's bedroom. When he was younger, Mars would give the zip line three hard shakes, which would vibrate the cable outside Caddie's window. That was their secret signal. Then Caddie would give three shakes back and zip over to the tree house right away. That was years ago.

Mars reached out now and shook the zip line three times. *One, two, three.* He wondered if the zip line would fall down, it was so old. Would Caddie come? Would it work?

He waited and waited. And then: *one, two, three.* Caddie was shaking the zip line back. She'd gotten the message! She was on the way! He heard the familiar sound of the trolley seat whipping down the zip line, and then a bump as Caddie reached the tree house, her feet jumping onto the platform.

"Mars?" she whispered. "Is that you?"

She crawled inside and saw him sitting on the floor.

"It *is* you!" she exclaimed. "Did you just get here? I sensed you. Then I thought, don't be crazy, Caddie. Mars Patel is not in your backyard. And *then* I felt the zip line shake. What are you doing here? We haven't used this place in years. I hope it doesn't fall apart."

"I'll take my chances," Mars said. "My mom says we're moving to Cleveland. Tomorrow."

"What! Oh no, Mars." Caddie looked shocked. "You can't move away."

"I know. Try telling her that. She thinks Port Elizabeth is a bad influence. She's mad I got expelled. But Fagan has had it in for me for a long time."

"She hates all of us," Caddie said. "I got another month of detention for skipping the GIFT test. Now my mom's so upset she says I can't leave my room for a month!"

Mars leaned back against the tree house wall. "Man, this sucks. Here I am expelled, you're stuck in your room . . . and we were supposed to go to the dance tonight."

"Well . . ." Caddie said slowly. "I'm still going."

"I thought you were grounded!"

"I know. But my mom is so desperate for me to be normal, she'll do anything, like making me go to this dance." Caddie sat wrapping her arms around her knees.

"Then you're going to the dance by yourself?"

"Nooo . . ." She looked away, embarrassed. "My mom is in this book club with Clyde Boofsky's mom and . . ."

"No way!"

"I'm sorry, Mars. I know you don't like him. But my mom and his mom are friends and . . ."

"Clyde is the biggest jerk," Mars said.

"Isn't he?" Caddie agreed, grimacing. "I'm only going because my mom is letting me out of the house this one evening. I'd much rather go with you."

Mars leaned forward. "Then you will. I'll meet you there."

"But you're expelled," Caddie said. "How will you even get in?"

"I promised you, right? I'll find a way."

"I guess you always do think of something, Mars." She seemed to read his mind because she added, "Of course you're better than Clyde. Who would like the Boof?"

"His mom," Mars said.

She laughed. "OK, I have to go, Mars. My mom will want to check on me to see if I'm ready."

"I'll be here a little longer. There's something I need to do first."

"Are you sure you'll be OK? You want me to bring you anything?"

Mars shook his head. "Nah. I got my phone and my coat, and it's dry in here. I'll see you later at the dance, Caddie. Everything will be OK."

"I know. We're a team, right?" She climbed out of the tree house, and a few seconds later, he could hear her zip-lining back to her room.

Mars took out his phone. He needed to talk to LIL. Soon.

## Caddie · JP

Caddie

which shoes r better for the dance

wedges or flats?

JP

don't know cads

I can't even match my socks!!

Caddie

ur coming right

JP

I hate dances

Caddie

but mars will b there and he's MOVING

JP

rly????

Caddie

to Cleveland

JP

yo mars can't survive without us!!!

Caddie

Now u have to come to the dance

JP

how do u feel

Caddie

sad :(

JP
I mean how do u feel feel
is the dance safe

Caddie
I didn't want to tell u
my head rly rly hurts

Caddie
oops gotta go mom knocking

## FROM THE PODCAST

Podcast listeners, I told you about drones.

Let me tell you something else.
There's no point trying to outrun them.
They will only find you faster!

There's one person who needs to know this.
So who is going to tell him?

To the stars!

### 610 Comments ⊗

**jerseyshores**     45 min ago
I heard mars has a plan to take over

**oreocookies**     33 min ago
someone needs to stand up to OP

**allie_j**   30 min ago
if we help mars does that mean we're against OP

**galaxygenius**     23 min ago
remember #missingkids

allie_j   9 min ago
**guyz I hear a buzzing noise**

lostinlondon   2 min ago
**u have to be careful about the drones**

## 20
# LOST AND FOUND

**T**he first thing Mars noticed when he got to the school was the line of security people guarding the front entrance. "Are you kidding me? Why does a school dance need so much security?"

"They're worried about another incident like Caddie's wolf announcement," Toothpick said. "I was reading online that it cost the school a lot of money because of the SWAT team they called in. Not to mention the bad publicity and pissed parents. And also, because you're a wanted man."

"Who, me?" Mars said, surprised. "Caddie's the one who did the announcement."

"Yeah, well no one knows that. But remember Oliver Pruitt, the world's richest person with diabolical intentions? He's on a mission to destroy you."

Mars glanced above him, where the same drone that

had been following him all evening was still hovering. "Don't remind me." He stared at the guards. "There must be a way to get in without getting seen."

"Of course," Toothpick said. "There's the door through detention. No one remembers that entrance because it isn't used anymore, and it's in the back where there isn't a security camera."

"Toothpick, you're a genius!" Mars exclaimed. "Let's go."

Several minutes later, Mars and Toothpick were inside the school and making their way up the metal staircase. Just as they were entering the sixth-grade hall, they ran into Mr. Q.

"Mars Patel, what are you doing here?" he demanded. "You know you're expelled, right?"

"Mr. Q, I promised Caddie that I'd go to this dance with her," Mars said. "I don't break my promises. Especially to my friends. Also, this might be the last time I see her. My mom is moving us to Cleveland."

"Cleveland!" Mr. Q said. He paused. "That's extreme."

"Don't you see?" Mars asked. "Will you please help me out this one last time?"

"Mr. Mars, you'd be surprised what I'd do for you." Mr. Q said softly. "Go on. I'll pretend I never saw you, all right? But stay out of sight of the chaperones. I can't promise what they'll do."

"Mr. Q—you are the boss," Mars said.

Toothpick nodded. "You're for real."

They hurried down the hall to the gym doors.

"See, your suspicions about Mr. Q were unfounded," Toothpick said.

"Yeah," Mars agreed. "I was wrong about him. He really came through." They opened the gym door. "Now to find Cad—" he stopped.

"Whoa, do you see Caddie?" Toothpick asked.

"Yeah," Mars said. "She looks . . . amazing."

Caddie was wearing a dark red chiffon dress with a scooped, beaded neckline that sparkled where the light hit it. Her hair was wavy and she wore glittery shoes to match the glittery frames of her glasses. She was talking to Clyde, who loomed over her in his misbuttoned shirt and wrinkled cargo pants.

"Randall!" Epica came gliding up to them. Gone was her blue blazer. She was wearing a spaghetti-strap white dress that poofed above her knees and her three-inch heels. "You look hot!"

Toothpick grinned. "You look dope, Epica. Would you like to dance?"

"I'd love to!"

Mars watched, agog, as Epica and Toothpick walked off to the dance floor.

By now JP had joined Mars.

"What just happened?" Mars said. "Did Toothpick just leave me to dance with a girl?"

"Bro, it looks that way," JP said. "I guess we should be happy for him, huh?" They watched Toothpick bust a move with Epica. "It's either that or bopping Epica on the head."

Mars looked at JP. "Hey, wait a minute, you're here. I thought you hate dances."

"I do," said JP, who was wearing a black sequined track suit. "Did you see Caddie?"

"Yeah."

"Did you see how good she looks?"

"Yeah." Mars sighed. "And I also saw the Boof with her."

By now, Clyde had taken Caddie to the dance floor, where he was dancing awkwardly, his arms and legs moving in a jerky motion, while Caddie had a polite smile plastered to her face, pretending to dance only when he looked at her.

"He's a disaster, Mars. Look at him!" JP exclaimed. "There's no competition."

"But she's with him, not me, thanks to her mom," Mars said glumly.

JP and Mars watched as the music changed to hip-hop and Clyde pumped his fists back and forth like he was driving a car. Caddie looked mortified. Next to him, Toothpick and Epica were doing some complicated pop-and-lock move. When had they gotten so good? Meanwhile, Clyde stumbled over Caddie's feet and landed on his knees.

"Oh my god, poor Caddie," JP said. "What are you doing here, Mars? Go over there! Ask Caddie to dance before she dies of embarrassment."

Mars nodded. "You're right, JP. I can do this, right?"

JP pointed to Caddie. "That way, dude."

Mars steeled himself. Never mind what Clyde or anyone else thought. Caddie really did look beautiful. And there was also something he'd never seen before: her in a crowded room, not being overwhelmed with all the noise and lights and other people, wondering when she could get away from it. That Caddie was gone. This Caddie looked like could take care of herself. Like she could do anything.

His thoughts flickered to Aurora. He'd always thought his first dance would be with her. That one day he'd work up the nerve to ask her and somehow, she'd say yes. But Aurora was gone, and his life had literally changed overnight. Now here he was, about to ask Caddie to dance with him. He still missed Aurora so much, yet he was glad to be with Caddie. Was that possible? And OK?

He took a deep breath. "All right, JP," he said. "Wish me luck."

"Break a leg. Or whatever they say."

Just then Mars's phone pinged.

"Ignore it," JP said immediately. "Now's your chance. The Boof went to get a drink."

Mars hesitated. "Let me just look." He pulled out his phone and saw the message on his home screen. "No way, JP," he exclaimed. "It's LIL, finally. I've been trying to reach her and now she sent me a link! She says it contains the location where we can find all the missing children."

"*All* of them?" JP crossed their arms. "You mean, like, in one place?"

"That's what it sounds like. Which means Aurora and Jonas, too, doesn't it?" Mars clicked the link. "Shoot. I'm not getting a strong enough signal here to download it. I'd have to go outside to get the link to open. But that means leaving the dance." He wavered.

It had taken an awful lot to get inside the school. If he went outside now, he might not be able to get back in. And Caddie was there, thinking he was coming. But what if the link solved the mystery at last? How long could he afford to wait? Any minute someone might find him—Oliver, one of the security guards, or worse, his mother.

JP saw Mars's face. "Look, I'll tell Caddie to wait for a few minutes. You go out and check the link, then come right back inside. That way you won't be thinking about it all night like I know you will."

"Thanks, JP," Mars said gratefully. "You're the best! I'll be back in five. I promise."

"Yeah, you better."

The air felt cool as Mars stepped out of the gym. Of course he would get back in. He'd done it before; he'd do it again. Just one link, right? Could this be the answer he was looking for? Just think: if he found Aurora and Jonas, maybe his mom would see what he'd been trying to do all this time. Maybe she'd change her mind about Cleveland. Maybe the school would let him back in, too. Who knows, maybe the newspapers and TV stations would all want to know how he'd solved the mystery of the missing kids around the world, and he'd finally meet LIL and find out why she was willing to help. And then Caddie and he would . . . well, one step at a time.

When Mars got outside the school, it was strangely quiet as he made his way to the parking lot. It took him a few minutes to realize that it was because the drone was gone. Already he was so used to it, that the whirring had become a part of the background air, like traffic or rain drumming across the tops of cars and rooftops.

But now the drone was gone. And so were the guards. In the parking lot, for the first time, Mars was completely alone. He breathed in and out, feeling the quiet night calm him. *This is how it should be*, he thought. *This is how*

*it used to be. Quiet. Alone. Not looking over your shoulder.*
He took out his phone and found the text from LIL.

### LIL · Mars

Fri, Oct 23, 7:38 pm

LIL (Lost in London)
**Click this, it's what you're looking for: https://yfxmp2g**

As he was about to follow the link, a sudden sound disturbed the air.

Mars's eyes darted up. "Hey!" he said.

The movement was swift—he felt himself in the air, almost weightless. Above him, he noticed the moon for the first time, peeking from behind an opaque cloud. It was a silver, crescent moon, like a boomerang going nowhere. His phone fell from his hands. He heard it thud on the asphalt.

"My phone . . ." he called out.

It was the last thing Mars said before he disappeared.

🎧

**Caddie was the one to find the phone. In the gym, she'd** sensed Mars as soon as he came in. Then she'd seen him talking to Toothpick and JP. The whole time her head had been throbbing, worse than it ever had, but she was getting better at not showing it. She didn't want Mars to notice. In fact, she'd been afraid to approach him. She knew that he and Clyde hated each other, and the last thing she wanted was a confrontation. Mars wasn't even supposed to be at the dance.

When Mars had left the gym, she'd known it was a mistake. She'd followed quickly, not even pausing to talk to Toothpick or JP, walking past the protesting chaperone who said Caddie wouldn't be able to come back in once she'd left the dance, and headed straight for the parking lot. It hadn't taken long for Caddie to find the phone. It was the only phone at H. G. Wells and possibly the entire state of Washington that was maroon with planets and stars covering the back. And it had been lying abandoned on the cracked asphalt of the parking lot that H. G. Wells Middle School still hadn't fixed, despite all the money they had poured into their security and surveillance systems. The same system with all those security videos that should have shown where Mars had gone, but instead would seem to suggest later that he had never been on the school premises, as if someone had erased him from the feed.

Caddie stooped down in her red chiffon dress and held the phone up to her ear. Nothing. It was on . . . Mars had been here only seconds ago. The text to LIL was still open with an expired link.

She clicked to send a voice message.

"I don't know who you are, LIL," she said, her voice

wavering only slightly. "Mars was here and now he's gone. I don't know where he is." She pushed up her glittery-framed glasses, the pair she always secretly wanted to wear but never did until today. Behind her an owl hooted and the night was clear. "But we're going to find Mars," she said. "His friends . . . and me."

# The Unexplainable Disappearance of Mars Patel

**Port Elizabeth, WA**—Late Friday evening, unconfirmed sources reported the disappearance of eleven-year-old Port Elizabeth resident Manu "Mars" Patel. Patel was last seen at the H. G. Wells Middle School dance, despite having been recently expelled for disruptive behavior and criminal activity, followed by the failure to report for mandatory GIFT testing administered annually by the school.

"We've never had a case like him," said Principal Dorena Fagan. "We have our ways of correcting deviant behavior, but Mars breached them all. Unfortunately, he's missing, but I can't say it was unexpected."

"Mars isn't like the other kids," said Mr. Quartz, a school aide. "That much I can say. Hope they find him."

The issue was first reported by friends who observed the young man missing during the school dance. Caddie Patchett, a friend, was able to recover Mars's cell phone but has not been able to locate or speak to him.

"It's not just him," she said to reporters at the *Gazette* office. "There are lots of kids missing. But Mars is the last straw. Someone has to do something about it. Now."

A formal search, which would need to be enacted by a legal guardian, has not yet been implemented. So far, the boy's mother, Saira Patel, has been unavailable for comment. ∎

## Caddie · Mars

Caddie

it's been five days since ur gone

JP and Pick look at me for answers

but I don't have any

I'm not u

Caddie

wish I could feel what ur thinking

it would rly help

Caddie

did u find what u were looking for in the parking lot

Caddie

I know u can't read these texts

Caddie

but I have a plan

I'm making it up as I go

15 ▶ 30

Gentle listeners,
I know there are reports going around about missing kids.
Well, the world is full of missing kids.
The question is knowing the difference between
missing kids who are missing
and missing kids who are up to something!

In the meanwhile, not everybody has a plan.
And not everybody has a good plan.

Mars Patel had a plan. See where that got him.
His friend Caddie has a plan, too.
Where do you think that will get her?

To the stars!

**899 Comments** ⊘

allie_j   15 min ago
I heard mars is missing #missingkids

oreocookies    11 min ago
mars stood up to OP that's why

galaxygenius    10 min ago
we need to find the #missingkids NOW

neptunebaby    8 min ago
who cares the planet's ending

allie_j   6 min ago
galaxy—how will we find the #missingkids we need a plan

lostinlondon    5 min ago
you have to look in the right place

# 21
# THE WHITE SUITS ARE HERE

**E**very afternoon after detention, Caddie, Toothpick, and JP climbed the fire escape to Mars's apartment to see if he had returned home. For JP it was a breeze climbing up the branch of the nearby tree and jumping onto the fire escape. For Caddie and Toothpick, it was another story. They weren't nearly as strong, so Toothpick came up with the idea to use the rope ladder that had come with his camp equipment.

"But Pick, you and your family don't go camping," JP said.

"We want to," Toothpick said. "We just never have. We've bought all the equipment."

The first time, JP had climbed up and tied the rope ladder to the fire escape, then Toothpick and Caddie climbed up afterward. So far they hadn't been able to get into the apartment, but they could look in through the window, and what they saw were boxes and boxes. Then every day, there were fewer boxes until there was only one box left.

"Are you sure we should keep doing this?" JP asked Caddie on the fifth afternoon when they met at the bottom of the fire escape. "So far we haven't found anything. And where's Pick? He disappeared after detention."

"I'm here already." Toothpick leaned over the railing from the top. "And you're late."

JP scowled. "How can we be late when all we're doing is counting boxes?"

"We want to go somewhere later. Right, Randall?" A second face peered over the railing.

"Epica!" JP exclaimed.

"I thought there was someone else up there," Caddie said. "I could sense it. What are you doing up there, Epica?"

"Randall invited me," Epica said. "He says you guys are always late and he needed company."

JP and Caddie climbed up to the landing.

"Why on earth would he call her?" JP muttered under their breath.

"Because she's my girlfriend," Toothpick said. "We want to hang out."

Epica looked around the fire escape. "Kind of drafty. And hard to stand in my wedges."

"Then maybe you should leave," JP said.

Caddie suppressed a smile. "OK, so Toothpick, did you see anything different this evening?"

He shook his head. "That one box is still there. No one has come by."

"I don't get it," Epica said. "If Mars's mom is moving to Cleveland like Randall says, why not get a moving truck and move all the boxes at the same time? Seems like a drag."

"I think it's to avoid detection," Caddie said. "Maybe Mars's mom doesn't want anyone to know."

"So she's mailing boxes one at a time," Toothpick said. "Because a moving truck can be followed."

"Poor Mars," JP said. "He's been snatched, and now his mom is moving out all his stuff."

"Yeah," Caddie said. "He came to the dance even when he wasn't supposed to, just because he promised. Mars has come through for us. We need to do the same for him. We need to find out what happened to him."

"Guys," said Epica, who was looking through the window. "What about those people inside? The ones in the white suits? Are they, like, movers?"

Toothpick looked where she was pointing. "Those are not movers," he said. "Look at the logos on their coats. Pruitt Prep. They're working for Oliver Pruitt!"

"Oh my god, let's get out of here before they see us!" JP exclaimed.

"Too late," Toothpick said.

Inside, the people in the white suits had spotted Caddie,

Toothpick, JP, and Epica on the fire escape. They pointed at them and started toward the window.

"Oh no, guys, run!" Caddie said.

All of them scampered down to the bottom rung of the fire escape. The ground was several feet below.

Above them a voice cried out, "Stop!" One of the White Suits had reached Mars's fire escape.

"We have to jump, guys!" JP called out. "No time for the rope."

JP was the first to leap down. Caddie was next. She thought about the gym class, swimming pools, and all the places she was bad at jumping, and then she jumped anyway. The ground met her hard and gloriously. She'd done it! Toothpick jumped easily, then rolled out of the way. "That's how they do it in parkour videos," he said. He looked up. "You can do it, Epica."

"Randall, I can't jump in wedges," she wailed.

Toothpick smiled at her patiently. "I believe in you, Epi. Just don't look up, OK? They're gaining."

Epica groaned and jumped. She landed partly on Toothpick.

"That wasn't so bad, Randall," she said.

Just then they heard a bus rounding the corner. It screeched to a halt in front of them and the doors opened. "Get in! Get in!"

JP's eyes doubled in size. "Mr. Q?"

"Hurry—I know, they're almost at the bottom," Mr. Q said. "I'll explain later!"

All four kids dashed into the bus, and it pulled away just as the first of the White Suits made it to the ground. "Heyyy!" he yelled at them, and then his voice disappeared as the bus drove away.

Inside, Caddie collapsed on a seat while Epica checked to see whether her wedges were broken and Toothpick helped her. Meanwhile JP stared and stared at Mr. Q.

"Why are you driving this bus?" they demanded.

Mr. Q overtook a car to merge onto a busy boulevard ahead of them. "Because they're watching my car," he said.

"Who?" JP asked.

"It's complicated."

"We've got time," JP said. "What's going on?"

"How did you know where we were?" Toothpick said. "Tell us the truth."

At the stoplight, Mr. Q turned to look at them. His glasses were on crooked and his usually neatly combed hair was standing on end. "There's more to this story than I've told you. You're right. I'm here because I'm tracking you guys. I've been doing that for some time."

"Then Mars was right about you!" JP exclaimed.

"No! I'm on your side."

"You mean you're helping us?" Caddie asked. She watched Mr. Q. He seemed to be inside some kind of box, unreadable. Caddie realized then that she'd never really been able to tell what Mr. Q was thinking. So far, he'd never done anything fishy. Until now.

"How do we know we can trust you?" she asked.

"Sometimes you have to go with what you know, Caddie," Mr. Q said. "Have I ever done anything to earn your distrust? Think long and hard and you'll know the answer to that."

"Well, when he puts it that way . . ." Toothpick said.

"You've got to trust someone, dudes," Epica said. "Or who's going to trust you?"

"Thanks, Epica, but you literally have no idea what's going on," JP said.

"Listen, everyone, this is what I know," Mr. Q said. "And maybe you know it, too. Something's not right about Pruitt Prep. Something's been off about Pruitt Prep for a long time."

"Yeah, it doesn't exist," JP said.

The light changed and they could see the green signal reflect off Mr. Q's glasses as he started driving again. "Oh, it exists all right," he said. "You won't *believe* how it exists."

# 22

# CLOSE

**I**t seemed like they drove forever—past the wharf, past Captain John's Grill, which served the best mac and cheese Caddie had ever eaten, past the bowling alley, past Jonas's favorite arcade, up hilly streets, and then past Lookout Point, where you could see Mount Rainier on a clear day—and still they kept driving and driving.

"Where are we going?" Epica whined. "Let's step on it—Randall and I have plans. We didn't come for a Port Elizabeth bus tour!"

"Put a lid on it," JP growled. "You're not the only one on this bus with a life."

"I'd prefer you talk more respectfully to my significant other, JP," Toothpick said. "She's not used to our escapades, and we have been on this bus for seventeen minutes."

JP rolled their eyes. "So, where are we going, Mr. Q?

You still haven't told us anything about Pruitt Prep."

Caddie nodded. "We have a right to know." She could feel everyone's growing apprehension. It wasn't just the White Suits who'd almost got them but Mr. Q turning up when he had, just like he had at Gale Island. It was too many coincidences. On top of that, there was something about being stuck inside a bus, she decided, that made you want to go bonkers.

Finally Mr. Q pulled into a Safeway parking lot. He shut off the engine and turned to everyone. "Sorry, kids. I didn't want to stop until I was sure we'd lost them. We're safe now." He took out a brown paper bag. "Cookies, anyone?"

"Are those flaxseed?" JP asked.

"Chia," Mr. Q said. "Locally grown."

"Sorry, but no thanks!" JP said.

"I'll have one," Toothpick said.

"I guess I could try one, too," Epica said. "Anything Randall does. JP's a wuss."

"I'd like to wuss you," JP said darkly.

"That doesn't even make sense," Epica said.

"Everyone, *please*. Mr. Q, answer us: What does Pruitt Prep have to do with Mars disappearing?" Caddie was still trying to read Mr. Q, but he had a way of keep his feelings under the surface. Like, right now all she could tell was that he believed in local ingredients, and that the cookie he was eating was very satisfying. But there seemed to be something going on underneath: concern, doubts, and a growing impatience.

"Your friends aren't the first of my students to go missing," he said as he chewed his cookie.

"You know about the missing kids?" she asked, surprised.

"Sure. I've wanted to bust open the case for years. And it's not just Port Elizabeth."

"Oh my god, are you talking about the missing kids?" Epica jumped in. "It's HUGE. I've been reading about it."

"The last thing I showed Mars was a map of all the countries involved, based on the flyers," Toothpick said. "There are forty-eight so far."

"Whoa," JP said.

"Mr. Q, the point is," Caddie said, "we really want to find Mars, Jonas, and Aurora."

"And I get that," he said. "I know how badly you want to find your friends. In fact, that's why I tried to encourage Mars to keep looking for them. I tried to help whenever I could without drawing attention to us. But now you guys have stepped into more dangerous territory than you realize. This is too big for you."

"What do you mean?" Toothpick asked. "You mean because Mars's video went viral?"

"Hey, I saw that video," Epica said. "Three million views.

What gives? So Mars was mad at Oliver Pruitt. Who cares?"

"Oliver Pruitt cares! And now you guys are taking on Pruitt, the most powerful man on the planet." Mr. Q's eyes flashed. "You have no idea what he's capable of. The podcast? That's nothing. There is a lot more to him than you know about. You're no match." Mr. Q ate the last of his locally grown chia cookie. "I mean, look at you guys. How are you going to do it? You're just kids."

"Mars thought we could do it," Caddie said slowly.

"Yeah, well, look what happened to him," Mr. Q. returned. "If I were all of you, I'd go home and forget about Oliver Pruitt and his school. It's not worth it."

"But if he's the reason Mars is gone," JP said, "then shouldn't we go back to Pruitt Prep?"

"*Back* to Pruitt Prep?" Epica repeated. "When were you there before?"

"We weren't," Toothpick said. "The school doesn't exist, even though the website says it does."

"Toothpick, the school *does* exist," Mr. Q said. "But you shouldn't go back. It's too dangerous."

"Fagan is big on rules," Caddie said suddenly. "Pick, isn't there a rule she has that says we need to fill out a permission slip to travel anywhere with a teacher? Otherwise the teacher could get into big trouble."

"Yes, Caddie. It needs to be signed by our parents and include allergy information."

Mr. Q sighed. "I know where you're going with this, Caddie. Threats don't suit you."

"Then help us!" Caddie beseeched. "We have to go back to the island. Back to Pruitt Prep. You said it yourself. Mars could be there. They could all be there."

"You said you saw nothing there," Mr. Q replied.

"Well, we didn't try during the day." Caddie looked outside, where the afternoon sun hung above the horizon. "And there's still time. It isn't evening yet."

"Mr. Q could give us a ride to the ferry," Toothpick pointed out. "We *are* on a bus. Though I'm still not sure why."

"So I can take you home!" Mr. Q said. "Why else?"

"Pick's idea is better!" Caddie said. "Mr. Q, you could take us to the ferry."

"No," said Mr. Q. "No, I could not!"

"You said it yourself: you want to find those missing kids. So take us there. We have to go back to that island. On that island all three of us have special . . ." Caddie's voice trailed off.

"What?" Epica spoke up. "All if you have special what?"

Caddie was about to say *special powers*. But some things were best left unsaid.

"Determination, Epica!" JP cut in. "Special determination."

Epica blinked. "Boring," she said.

Meanwhile, something seemed to have changed Mr. Q's mind. He had started up the engine.

"Fine, kids. Buckle up," he said, relenting at last. "Next ferry leaves on the hour."

JP whooped. "You're a good man, Mr. Q."

Their teacher pulled the bus onto the road warily. "We'll see, JP."

🎧

**The Gale Island ferry was the strangest one Caddie had** ever seen. First of all, there was no room to drive your car on like the Bremerton ferry that went to Seattle, with multiple floors for passengers to sit and a lookout deck on both ends of the boat. This ferry was small, with only one floor for sitting, no observation deck, no vending machines in sight, and most of all, no one around who seemed to be controlling the ferry. Apparently Mr. Q, Caddie, and her friends were the only ones on the boat as it headed across the water.

Mr. Q said he would go downstairs to see if anyone was available in the control room.

"Well, this is weird," Caddie said.

"Yeah, nobody's around," JP said.

"I guess that's kinda like how your life is," Epica said, twirling a strand of hair around finger. "You know, empty with nobody there."

"Can you stop being so mean all the time, Epica?" Caddie said, losing her patience.

"Epica is scared inside," Toothpick said gravely, "and uses insults to push people away."

"Well, how about I push her away, too?" JP asked, making their hand into a fist.

"JP," Caddie said.

"Whatever," Epica said, but she took a step back from JP.

Just then the lights around them blinked, and a large image appeared in front of them.

"What's going on?" Epica stammered. "Who's that in front of us?"

"Not him again," Caddie said, sighing.

"I thought I pulled the plug," JP said, groaning.

"Don't worry, Epi, it's just a hologram!" Toothpick said. "Remember the assembly?"

Projecting in front of them was a grainy, wavering image of Oliver Pruitt holding a camera. This time he was dressed in a Hawaiian shirt, khaki shorts, and a straw hat. Kind of like he was on a beach vacation except without the sand. "Welcome aboard the USS *Pruitt*!" he announced cheerfully. "I am your holographic captain, Oliver Pruitt! By now, you must have observed the boat is automated. Not only that, your trip to Gale Island is being carefully monitored from Pruitt Prep Mission Control. We take security very seriously. Smile at the camera!"

"So much for the element of surprise," JP observed.

"I guess he knows we're coming," Caddie said glumly.

The holographic Oliver Pruitt smiled widely at them and continued taking pictures like a creepy tourist. "Smile!" he said again.

Epica gave a big sunny smile and tossed her hair back. "Will I be getting copies?" she asked.

"It's a recording, Epi," Toothpick said. "I think it's for their files."

"They better not upload my photo without a filter," Epica said. "I like sepia."

"Please note that the entrance to the school is strictly forbidden," Oliver Pruitt chirped. "Only students accepted through our GIFT testing protocols are allowed inside. Otherwise, trying to access the school is futile. We have twenty-four-hour surveillance, and the grounds are surrounded by twenty-foot titanium walls that are impenetrable—"

JP walked over, and a sudden crash interrupted the recording as their fist smashed the equipment. "Easy enough to penetrate the projector," JP said with satisfaction, observing that their fist showed no signs of injury. "Hey, guys, I'm stronger already!"

"JP!" Caddie warned.

"You shouldn't have done that," said Mr. Q, who'd just come up the stairwell.

"Yeah? Do you see anyone around here to stop me?" JP waved their arms around.

"Yes," came a thin, reedy voice. Behind Mr. Q stood one of the White Suits, holding a neutralizer dart. "You should have thought before destroying private property," the White Suit said. "Breaking the projector activated APES."

"APES? Like gorillas?" JP asked.

"The Autonomic Procedure for Emergency Situations," Mr. Q said blandly. "The boat is being automatically turned around to return to its last approved coordinates. We're going back to Port Elizabeth." His eyes traveled nervously to the neutralizer dart in the White Suit's hands.

"In the meanwhile, we have to neutralize the source of the problem," the White Suit said. He raised the dart to take aim.

Immediately the four kids ran through the automatic doors to the south deck.

"What do we do next, Caddie?" JP panted when they reached the mast. Behind them, the White Suit had just come out of the automatic door.

"Wait, me?" Caddie could feel the boat lurch as it turned around. "But I don't make the decisions. That's Mars."

"Mars isn't here," Toothpick said.

Caddie gulped. She felt woozy and faint, and time was running out.

"OK, we need a plan," she said.

"Maybe I can override the system?" Toothpick said. "I have tools in my backpack, and I'm already feeling smarter. But I need time."

Caddie nodded. "What else we got?"

Epica shrugged. "Can't you guys, like, swim?"

"Epica's right," Toothpick said. "We're not too far from shore, and it is low tide. Plus, my backpack is waterproof and doubles as a life preserver."

"Geez, Toothpick," JP said. "That doesn't change the fact that I HATE GETTING WET."

Caddie thought fast. "Let's do it," she said. JP opened their mouth, but Caddie cut them off. "JP, we're out of time. Look, that guy is getting ready to aim again. Hurry, we need a distraction!"

"Leave that to me!" Epica said suddenly. She reached down to remove a shoe. "I'll stay. You go!"

Caddie, Toothpick, and JP rushed to the edge of the boat. Over the railing, the water looked uninviting and cold. "It's now or never!" Caddie told them.

"Take that!" Epica yelled. The last thing Caddie saw was Epica on board, hurling her wedge at the White Suit.

"One, two, three!" yelled Caddie as she, Toothpick, and JP plunged into the sound.

They could hear Epica's words lingering in the air as they hit the water. "Randall, I love youuuu . . ."

∩

**Caddie crawled onto the gravelly shore of Gale Island.** Never had she been so glad to see sand. Even if it was inside her shoes, down her shirt, and in her ears.

On the sand next to her, JP was wet and mad but without a single scrape. On her other side, Toothpick was already calculating ahead. She could read his thoughts. He knew the lay of the island. The map was pretty much ingrained in his memory. Caddie was suddenly grateful. Toothpick's brain meant they would never get lost.

Ahead of them came the howling sound they all remembered. And something else. A whirring over their heads.

"Oh my god, not that animal," JP said. "We're back not three seconds and that thing is still on the loose."

"Shush, JP." Caddie squinted. "It's one of Pruitt's drones. It's spotted us already."

"Let it come at me, then," JP said. "I'm strong. I can smash it into a pulp."

"Maybe it's better to keep moving," Toothpick said.

"Toothpick's right," Caddie said, shivering. "Let's head for the trees. It can't follow us there."

They scrambled for the wooded area but JP went sprawling before they got there.

"Who left this junk here?" JP had tripped on something tossed on the ground. It looked like rolls of rubber hoses and tubes and shipping supplies.

"It's from the ferry," Toothpick said. The whirring above

them got louder. And this time something new happened. The drone started launching pellets at them.

"Are you serious?" JP yelled. "That drone is shooting at us?"

They ran until the three of them were inside the woods. They leaned over, catching their breath.

"I never thought I'd be shot by a drone," JP said, huffing.

"They weren't real pellets." Toothpick held up something in his hand. "See?"

JP looked. "It's hard to see in the dark, but is that a peanut?"

"Yep," Toothpick said. "I guess it's biodegradable."

"Oh, yay," JP said. "The drone is ecologically friendly . . . AND it wants to kill us."

"Let's get moving," Caddie said. "Pick, you know how to go, right?"

The three of them continued, trudging through the woods. As the excitement with the drone died down, Caddie tried to keep her distance so she wouldn't keep colliding with JP's and Toothpick's thoughts. Already she could feel JP wondering if they were walking into danger, and if JP could protect them all. Caddie could sense JP's hands balling up with determination.

Toothpick was determined, too. Everything in his mind was clear and precise, and his confidence kept growing. He *was* getting smarter. He knew the scientific names of the trees in front of them, he knew which direction was due north, and he'd already calculated an algorithm for how long it would take to skirt the entire island.

But sometimes his thoughts would stray, like thinking how brave Epica was for throwing her favorite shoes at the White Suit so they could get away. That was love, wasn't it? Plus Epica had looked so pretty in blue, and he liked the way she tilted her head when she said his name.

This is where Caddie stopped for a moment to let Tooth-pick go farther ahead. *Give the guy some privacy*, she told herself.

Just then, the howling started up again.

"Pick, where are we going?" JP asked. "Now would *not* be the time to get lost. I'm strong, but I'm not sure I can fend off starving wolves."

"Trust me. I see the entire island laid out in my head," Toothpick said. "We're very close."

"We were very close last time," JP said. "But the school wasn't there. What's different about this time?"

"Because it's here," Caddie said suddenly. She stopped, noticing the pulsing she felt inside her. It had been there, growing slowly. She wasn't shivering anymore. It was the school. She was feeling the school. "I can feel it," she said.

She was right. A few minutes later, the trees gave way to a clearing. The same clearing they'd run to last time. But last time it was completely empty. And now . . . now!

Caddie, Toothpick, and JP craned their necks.

"It's humongous!" Caddie breathed.

Humongous didn't even cover it. What was in front of them was unlike anything they had ever seen. The school was sleek and gorgeous, rising up from the ground like a missile. The walls were made of steel, the windows of reinforced glass, with two shorter towers flanking the central building, each topped with glass domes and metallic spires. And surrounding the structure was an immense wall twenty feet high that shimmered under the setting sun. This was the titanium wall that Oliver Pruitt had been talking about. What had he called it? Impenetrable. Impossibly strong and impossible to breach.

"It's here!" exclaimed Toothpick. "The labs, the towers, the titanium walls. I don't get it. How can it be here when it wasn't before?"

"Maybe it's a hologram," JP wondered. "Like Oliver."

Caddie leaned forward, pressing her palm against the titanium bricks. She was surprised by the warmth that spread through her like a jolt, almost as if the wall were alive.

"No, it's real," she said. She started to pull her hand back but left it lingering a little longer, enjoying its warmth. By now, Toothpick's thoughts were coming through to her, and this time they weren't about Epica. Instead, he was studying the walls, the two towers, the dizzying height of the main building, and he was hatching the most thrilling plan Caddie had known.

"Toothpick, you're a genius," she said. "Or crazy. Or both."

"Did you just read my mind?" Toothpick asked. "Then you tell JP. You're better at it."

"Tell me what, guys?" JP's eyes narrowed. "We're not getting on another boat, are we?"

"No. Toothpick has a plan," Caddie said. "I know you hate swimming, JP. But how do you feel about . . . flying?"

15 ▶ 30

Dear listeners:

Ever wonder what makes you who you are?

Is it the socks you wear? Your favorite band?

I believe what makes you YOU is your response when you're tested.

When the odds are stacked against you,

are you brave? Generous? A good friend?

If someone asks YOU to take the leap,

will you hide or will you FLY?

To the stars!

1.5 mil Comments ⊗

jerseyshores    30 min ago

**fly**

staryoda    18 min ago

**fly**

wanna_B    17 min ago
fly

godzilla    14 min ago
hide

allie_j    13 min ago
R we talking fly like a bird or fly like a plane

oreocookies    9 min ago
trick qtn don't answer

neptunebaby    8 min ago
everything is a trick qtn

epica_is_epic    6 min ago
this podcast sucks my babe and his friends kick butt

## 23

# WELCOME TO PRUITT PREP (NOT REALLY)

**T**he idea sounded even more unbelievable when Caddie said it out loud to JP: "We want to launch you into the school with tubing tied to a tree."

Toothpick pushed up his glasses. "Think of it as a human slingshot."

There. They'd said it. It was too crazy. Time for another idea.

But to Caddie's surprise, JP jumped up and down.

"I love it! You. Are. Brilliant!" JP slapped Toothpick on the back, and he grimaced. "Sorry, Pick. I forget my strength on this island!"

When JP was done gushing, Toothpick explained the finer details. With the proper angle and the right amount of tension, the rubber tubing they'd seen lying near the dock could be used to send JP flying fifty-five feet through the air, to land on the terrace of the south tower, where there was a door that could be opened from the outside. JP would take the staircase down six flights, pass the theater on the right, go through the sensory hall, and reach the south loading dock to let Toothpick and Caddie in.

"It's all there in the layout of the school, which I have memorized," Toothpick said.

"Six flights of stairs? Is that how tall the school is?" JP gazed up at the top of the building, which seemed to disappear into the clouds.

"No, that's how tall the north and south towers are," Toothpick said. "The highest part of the school is at the center—that's twenty floors."

"Twenty floors!" JP paled. "That's a lot of stories."

"Right, but we just have to get to the top of the south tower," Toothpick said. "Six floors. Not twenty. Just avoid the metal spire or you'll get impaled."

"OK . . ." JP said, a little unsurely.

"Trust me, JP," he said. "I have it all worked out. Come with me."

As JP followed Toothpick into the woods, Caddie said she wanted to check the wall again. "Maybe I can sense whether there's anyone on guard at the South Tower," she said.

As she walked around the wall, she held out her hand to feel the gleaming titanium again. It was so hard to resist. Every time she touched it, she was filled with a rush of happiness. The wall felt cold and hot at the same time, like it could be alive—but not like a human being. More like . . . the hood of a car after a drive. Then other sensations slowly began to tingle to the surface. People. Guards. Many of them. Surprised, she kept her hand still until she could separate out one of the people. It was a guard near the south side who was . . . hungry. How extraordinary it was, channeling his feelings . . . He wanted a sandwich; his stomach growled; he was going to take a break in five minutes. Wow. That was perfect. As she turned to go, there was something else she felt under her hand, a warmth that wasn't like a car engine but like a summer day or a good memory. She shivered, then finally lifted her hand.

When she returned to Toothpick and JP, she was surprised to find they had already gone back to the dock to retrieve the tubing, and the slingshot was done. Caddie watched as Toothpick inspected his work.

He pulled on the tubing tied to two trees. "See? It's good to go."

"Guess what else?" Caddie said. "The guard at the south tower is about to go on break."

"Then we need do it now, when nobody's there," JP said.

"Exactly," Caddie said. "Also . . . I felt Mars."

"For real?" JP asked.

"Yeah," Caddie said. "It means we're close, guys."

"I've adjusted the tension," Toothpick said, "and pointed the sling toward the south tower terrace, *away* from the spires. I checked the wind direction, too. We're ready."

A sudden whirring descended on them.

"Oh no, another drone!" Caddie cried.

"Don't worry, that's my pet drone, Droney," Toothpick said.

"What?" Caddie asked blankly. She looked from Tooth-pick to JP.

"Remember the drone that crashed into us at school?" JP asked. "Toothpick brought it with him in his backpack, and he took it out while you were looking at the wall. He reprogrammed it, and now it's working for us."

"I figured out how by watching a YouTube video," Tooth-pick explained.

"I don't believe it," Caddie said. "But with you, Pick, any-thing's possible."

"Welcome to another day on Weirdness Island," JP commented.

"Hey Droney, station yourself at the top of the south tower," Toothpick said.

"OK. Stationing myself at the top of the south tower," Droney responded.

"And if JP lands on the terrace, come tell us," Toothpick added.

"OK, I can do that," Droney added. Then it went flying up and over the wall.

"I never thought a drone could be your personal slave," JP said. "I thought it was just good for maiming people."

"Not if you know how to code," Toothpick said. He stood back. "Ready to launch."

"Don't put it like that!" JP said quickly.

"Why not? It is a launch."

"Yeah, but we're launching *me.*"

"Don't worry. You're going to be fine," Toothpick said. "Remember: on the island, you're indestructible. Which means nothing can hurt you, even if something goes wrong with this sling." He paused. "Well, at least I think so."

"Gee, that's so reassuring," JP said. "All right, let's go."

"Wait—JP," Caddie jumped in. "You're incredibly brave. I want you to know that. And a good friend."

JP smiled at her. "Mars would do it for me. That's what friends are for."

Caddie nodded. Thinking about Mars made her wish he was here. He was the one who could tell whether a plan would work. But he was the reason they were here in the first place. She just hoped she was making the right decisions. There was no way of knowing.

"And Cads, it will be fine," JP added.

"What do you mean?" she asked, flushing, because she knew what JP was going to say.

"I don't have to be a mind reader like you," JP said. "I

can tell you're worried, but you're a good leader. You know that, don't you? I'm proud of you."

"Thanks, JP," Caddie said. "Teamwork, right, guys?"

"Speaking of," Toothpick said, "Caddie, tell me again where to aim. You're better at feeling directions than I am. JP, get ready to launch."

"Quit saying that!"

"Fine, just say when."

"I'm proud of you, too, Toothpick," JP said. "OK, launch this puppy."

Caddie pointed. "That way. The guard is gone."

Toothpick and Caddie pulled back on the tubing. JP braced themself.

"Three, two, one, go!" Toothpick and Caddie let go of the tubing.

If Caddie hadn't known it was possible, she couldn't have imagined it—watching JP fly through the sky like an astronaut was amazing. A brilliant astronaut in a sparkly scarf. Caddie felt her breath catch in her throat. JP was yelling something. Caddie strained to hear, and then JP's words came to her: "To . . . the . . . stars . . ."

"Come on, Pick," Caddie said. "We need to get to the loading dock. Fast!"

∩

**It seemed like an eternity to Toothpick as they waited at the** loading dock after JP had catapulted into the school. The whole time he'd been designing and implementing his contraption, he'd been sure it would work. It was amazing how all the pistons in his brain were firing, that as soon as he thought of a question, he already knew the answer to it.

It was his heart that was having a hard time keeping up. When he'd seen JP sailing through the air, his reaction had been completely different from Caddie's. He hadn't seen an astronaut taking flight. He'd seen his best friend possibly flying to their doom. His anxiety rose exponentially while he and Caddie waited. What if he had been overconfident? What if JP hadn't landed on the terrace but overshot, or undershot, or headed straight to the metal spire and . . .

"Where is Droney?" Toothpick asked nervously. "He should be back by now. Why isn't he back yet? Can you sense what happened like you did with the guards or Mars?" he asked Caddie. "Can you tell where JP is? Or Droney?"

Caddie shook her head. "I'm sorry, Pick. I'm not getting anything anymore. No Mars, no guard, no JP. Maybe it's because I was near the wall before? Or because JP is inside the school and too far away? Or because . . ." She stopped. They both had an image of the metal spires.

Toothpick shuddered as they stood in silence for a few terrible moments.

At last came a familiar whir.

"Droney!" Toothpick exclaimed. "You're back! Did JP make it inside?"

"Your friend landed on the south tower terrace," Droney reported.

"Was JP hurt?" he asked.

"Not possible to confirm," Droney said.

"Did anyone see JP?" he asked.

"Not possible to confirm," Droney repeated.

"Is JP coming to let us in?"

"Not possible to confirm," Droney chirped a third time.

"I think we have to wait, Pick," Caddie said. "Some things Droney can't tell us."

"'Only two things are infinite, the universe and human stupidity, and I'm not sure about the former.' Quote by Albert Einstein," said Droney.

"Wow, a quoting drone," Caddie said.

"And I think he just called us stupid," Toothpick said.

Just then, the door to the loading dock opened.

"JP!" Toothpick rushed in, with Caddie and Droney following him.

Toothpick had never been so happy to see JP in his life. Words came to his lips and abandoned him as he wrapped his arms around his friend.

"Pick, I—" JP couldn't finish. "Hey, buddy, you're hugging me too tight!" JP's voice broke off as Toothpick held on. "Pick!"

"I was afraid you weren't going to make it," Toothpick

said at last, his voice muffled. "I'm smarter on this island, but I'm making more mistakes, too."

"Droney did say JP reached the top," Caddie said softly.

"Confirmed," said Droney.

"Yeah, but I'm the one who programmed him," Toothpick said. "What if he was wrong? No offense, Droney."

"Droney?" repeated a familiar voice.

For the first time, Caddie became aware of her surroundings—a darkened hallway with a touch-screen wall on one side. The floor was sparkling white even in the dark hall. A gray conveyor belt was moving packages with robotic arms at the far end of the hall. But it was the voice that got her attention. The voice she hadn't heard in days.

"I wanted to tell you," JP said. "Look who I met on the way down."

"Wassup, peeps? Long time no see! That there your drone? Crazy stuff." He was his same tall, lanky self, minus his baseball cap.

"Jonas!" Caddie said, relieved.

But before anyone could say more, there was a tremendous sound, as if the whole world were crumbling apart, and then the entire building began to shake.

# 24

# LEFT RIGHT

addie was convinced the ceiling would collapse on top of her and crush her. She instinctively curled into a ball and covered her head. But just as soon as the building shook, it stopped shaking.

"What was THAT?" burst JP.

Toothpick was scratching his head. "We are near the Cascadia subduction zone."

"Cascadia what zone?" JP repeated. "Droney, translate."

"Sure, I can do that," Droney said. "The Cascadia subduction zone is a fault line that runs from Canada to California, through the Seattle and Puget Sound area."

"Fault line? What does that mean?" JP's voice went up a notch.

"Droney is talking about earthquake zones," Toothpick explained. "We are in the middle of one. All of Western Washington is, including Gale Island and Port Elizabeth."

"Are you saying we were in an earthquake just now?" JP gasped.

Jonas smiled peaceably. "Relax, guys. Follow me." He began walking down the hallway.

They hurried to catch up with Jonas's long strides.

*"Relax?"* JP repeated. "How can you say that when you were kidnapped and taken against your will to this school? And it doesn't even exist half the time!"

"And were we in an earthquake just now?" Caddie demanded. "What's going on?"

Jonas kept walking. "Soon it will all be clear. Come on, this way. It's shorter." He opened the door. "By the way, it's a little windy in here."

Jonas turned a wheel on a steel door to unlock it, and then pulled it open.

When they stepped inside, a sudden gale threatened to knock them over. Droney skittered above them as they found themselves suddenly traversing a rocky terrain.

"Whherrrre . . . arrrre . . . weee?" JP's voice got lost in the wind.

"Don't talk," Jonas said. He braced himself against the windstorm that blew through the cavernous room.

Caddie could hardly keep her eyes open unless she kept them pointed down. There were desert rocks and sandy crevices along the ground, making it hard to walk. She struggled to put one foot in front of the other. The only

237

thing she could do was follow Jonas's figure right in front of her.

The wind continued, and somewhere they heard it again, the howling sound, but this time it was much, much closer. *It's coming from inside,* she thought. *It's coming from . . .*

Caddie stopped, rooted in terror.

It was coming from the creature a few feet ahead of her.

Never had she seen such a thing. Several feet tall, armored, long, grotesque legs stretching out in all directions. It was watching them with its many eyes, its mouth sprawled open and ravenous. What she saw was an enormous spider plated in steel.

Her voice died in her throat.

"Come this way." Jonas's voice echoed in front of her. "Don't stop now."

The wind was at her back. She could barely see or feel anything but the horror of the creature before them. Somewhere she felt a hand on her arm. JP? Toothpick? Through the wind and darkness, she moved forward, passing the creature, not sure what would happen next.

Impossibly, a door closed behind her. Jonas was turning another wheel, round and round, sealing it shut. They leaned against the wall, breathing hard.

Caddie pushed her hair out of her face. They were all

there: Toothpick, JP, Jonas, and even, whirring above them, Droney.

"You call that 'a little windy'?" JP panted. "First an earthquake, then a tornado, and then that—that—*thing*! Jonas, what are you trying to do, kill us?"

Jonas continued to smile. Caddie had thought the creature inside that strange room was scary, but now seeing her friend's smile was scarier. Also, why could she not sense any of his thoughts or feelings? It was like Jonas was a blank slate.

"Jonas?" she whispered.

He nodded sunnily. "That's my name. Listen, that was no tornado, just a wind simulator. We went through that room 'cause it was a shortcut. Now we're almost where we need to be. Just keep following me."

Toothpick pushed up his glasses. "OK, Jonas. Whatever you say. Let's go."

JP looked at Toothpick in surprise. As soon as Jonas was a few paces ahead, Toothpick whispered, "I've figured it out. He's been brainwashed."

"I knew you were thinking that," Caddie whispered. "I wish I could read Jonas's mind, too, but he's all closed off."

"What do we do, Cads?" JP whispered.

"Shh. Just do what he says until we come up with a better plan," Caddie said in a low voice.

They turned down a hallway with what looked like doors to classrooms on either side.

"Keep walking," Jonas called behind him.

As they walked by each door, Caddie wondered what was going on inside each room. She could feel activity, but this felt like people moving around, not strange scary creatures, their thoughts coming at her faintly through the thick, reinforced walls. Some of the thoughts were unrecognizable until Caddie thought she detected some French. Were those foreign languages she was sensing? Curiosity finally got the better of her. She lingered behind everyone until she was standing in front of a door.

Inexplicably, it opened.

A teenager in a long flowing tunic and pants stood there. Their brown hair was short, cut above their ears, and the teen wore a nose ring. "Namaste," said the person, looking Caddie up and down. "Are you here for training?"

Behind them, several other teenagers milled around a large table that spanned nearly the length of what looked like an enormous classroom. Hundreds of voices buzzed in different languages. Perched on the table was a large wheel that seemed to be spinning of its own accord. Several teens were pointing to it with great excitement. A few lines of English and other languages broke through.

"That's the wrong angle. Tilt it!"

"It's gaining speed!"

"But we haven't tested out the formula!"

"*Pardon! Je sais quels numéros utiliser!*"

"*Achtung!*"

Caddie felt dizzy and enthralled all at once. So many voices, so many thoughts! And they were all coming fast, just like the rapidly spinning wheel that was hovering over the table and was now taking flight across the room. The teenagers cheered, their faces shining faintly with perspiration. All of them had their hair cut short, just like the one who opened the door. It was impossible to tell who was a boy or girl or what. But they looked shiny and beautiful in their flowing tunics. Caddie felt herself being drawn to them, like a magnet was pulling her into the room.

"There you are!" Jonas's voice jabbed from behind.

Caddie jumped, startled.

"Sorry, Numi, this one is with me." Jonas gave the teen-ager at the door his standard smile.

"OK, Jonas," said the teen. "Come back later when you're ready!"

"Will do, Numi," Jonas said, pulling Caddie along with him.

Behind them, the door closed. Ahead, JP and Toothpick were waiting.

"Where did you go, Cads?" JP asked.

"That was the inventor room, Caddie," Jonas said. "It

can get pretty intense there. Better stick with me. Now isn't the time to stray."

Stray! Caddie followed Jonas wordlessly the rest of the way. She was still feeling the glow from the young people in the room, and regret ebbed through her that she'd had to leave them. They all looked so happy.

Caddie shook her head, trying to clear her thoughts. She wasn't being herself.

"OK, this time, nobody go away," Jonas said. He had brought them to another hall. He held a finger to his mouth. "And you've got to be quiet."

Caddie, Toothpick, and JP fell silent. Now what was going on?

From below, a sound became louder and louder until Caddie recognized it: the sound of marching. One, two, one, two. Left, right, left, right. The marching continued steadily, getting closer to them until they saw who was marching. Lines and lines of kids in white suits, marching single file down the hall on the lower floor of the atrium.

Caddie gasped. In the room with Numi, it hadn't occurred to her, but now, from a distance, seeing so many more children filling the hallways than she could count, the idea came crashing like a brick. Caddie knew Toothpick and JP were thinking the exact same thing as her.

The missing children.

Marching in the hallway and back in the inventor room.

And maybe the whole school. Why were they here at Pruitt Prep?

Caddie studied the kids marching past in the atrium. They seemed younger than the ones in the inventor room. Their hair wasn't cut short, and instead of tunics, they wore white suits. Not only that, each child held a small digital pad on which they seemed to be furiously scribbling equations and plugging in formulas as they marched. Were the children marching . . . or solving problems? It looked like a little of both. And on every child's face was an expression of rapt attention, like the people in the inventor room. They were all having . . . *fun.*

After what seemed like forever, the last of the marching kids turned down the hall and disappeared, their stomping feet slowly fading away.

"That's our junior league of problem solvers," Jonas said.

"But are those the missing kids?" Caddie pressed. "And the ones in the inventor room . . ." She tried to get the answer from Jonas's mind, but still she could read nothing but mush. Gone were the video games and batting averages. Jonas's brain was still a blank slate. "You have to tell us something, Jonas. We can't wait anymore."

Jonas was punching a code into a wall next to a door. "Patience, dudes," he said. "This is where it all becomes clear. Come inside."

Caddie was about to refuse, but when she looked in, she suddenly felt herself relax. Inside was a carpeted game room with potted palm trees dotting the corners and soft, upholstered couches around a big, fluffy rug. There was a juice machine, a table with snacks laid out, and a large TV screen on the wall. The air smelled sweet and fruity.

"Sustenance," Jonas said, grinning.

This grin looked a little more like the old Jonas.

"Well, OK . . ." Caddie said uncertainly, frowning. "But you still haven't told us anything, Jonas, and . . ."

JP dove for the couch and a bag of chips. "Man, I'm starving. I could use a little TLC."

In the back, Toothpick was examining the pool table equipped with cue sticks and a full set of balls ready to go. "Mahogany and chrome," he said. "Nice."

"OK," Jonas said. "Catch you later."

"Wait, what?" JP asked from the couch.

Before anyone could say anything, Jonas had exited through the door. There was a sound of a metal arm sliding across on the outside.

"He's locked us in!" Caddie said. "I knew something was wrong. Why didn't I sense this coming?"

JP stood up. "He can't do that. This is so wrong."

"Droney, is there any way to get out?" Toothpick asked.

"I can answer that for you," Droney said. "There is an access pad at the door."

"Great—can you open the door?" Toothpick asked.

"Negative," Droney said. "The access code has been deactivated by the last user. That would be your friend Jonas Hopkins."

"Not our friend anymore," JP muttered. "Didn't he just leave us here?"

"That's not the real Jonas, locking us in," Toothpick said. "It's his brainwashed self, who's doing someone else's bidding."

"Why would he lock us in?" JP asked. "Caddie, use your feels. We're all out of options."

Caddie was on the couch, her eyes closed, fingertips at her temples. This was such an unsettling room, fully insulated, no windows, and no sensations of any kind. At first all she could feel was herself and her friends locked inside its steel walls. But then there was something else, something distant, that warm feeling again. It was out there; it had been there all along. And it was . . . it was . . . was that possible? Coming closer? There were beeping sounds outside the door. Someone was punching in a code from the outside.

"Someone's coming in!" JP announced.

Caddie opened her eyes and looked up.

The door opened.

Caddie jumped up. She ran to him. They all did.

He was wearing the same outfit he had been wearing

at the dance before he disappeared. His face was smooth, unworried; he even seemed to glow. His eyes took in everyone. Then he spoke.

"You made a big mistake," Mars said blandly. "You shouldn't have come."

## 25
# EIGHTY MILES A SECOND

I t looked like Mars. It talked like Mars. But the words that came out of his mouth?

*You shouldn't have come.*

Those sounded like someone from another planet.

"Uh, nice to see you, too, Mars," JP said sarcastically, but more hurt than anything.

Toothpick was more direct. "We thought we'd never see you again," he said.

"Mars, are you OK?" Caddie asked cautiously. Why couldn't she sense what he was thinking? All his thoughts were gone. It was just like Jonas.

"I'm great, Caddie," Mars pronounced. "Never been better!"

"Never been better?" JP said incredulously. "How did you get here? Did they kidnap you?"

Mars motioned them to come with him down the

hallway. With reluctance, they followed him, looking at one another in bewilderment.

"Don't you *love* how the walls open?" Mars asked, beaming. "Come on, guys. That's right. I need you to keep following me!"

JP, Caddie, and Toothpick lagged behind.

"What's happened to him?" JP whispered. "That's not Mars!"

"Maybe they've brainwashed him, too," Toothpick whispered. "And he's now a zombie."

"Can we trust him? What if he's taking us straight to Pruitt?" JP asked.

Caddie frowned. "Mars isn't acting like himself. But what choice do we have?"

"To not follow him!"

"Odds are better if we stay with Mars," Toothpick said quietly.

In front of them, the doors of an elevator suddenly opened.

"Come on!" Mars called out. "The elevator doesn't stay open forever!"

The rest of them shuffled inside. JP was scowling, Toothpick was fidgeting, and Caddie was thinking so hard she almost ran into a wall. Droney hovered next to all of them.

"Oh, drones are not allowed inside the elevator," Mars said.

"He's mine," Toothpick said. "I reprogrammed him."

Droney made a clicking sound.

"It's OK, Droney," Toothpick said. "We're not leaving you behind, right?"

"Slight deviations from protocol are accepted with authorization," clipped Droney.

Mars sighed. "Very well. I can make an exception this one time." He punched some numbers into the wall of the elevator. "OK, everyone, hold on."

The doors closed. Suddenly the compartment began to climb, accelerating rapidly up the elevator shaft.

"H-how fast i-s-s this thinnng?" JP asked. Their fingers were coiled around the hand railings.

"Pretty fast," Mars said.

"It's a high-speed lift," Toothpick explained, his voice wavering with the speed. "How fast are we going, Droney?"

"Fifty miles per second," Droney answered. "And accelerating."

"I think I'm going to be sick," Caddie said. She closed her eyes, trying not to think about the last meal she'd eaten.

"Almost there," Mars said cheerfully.

"Now eighty," Droney added.

"Where are we going, Mars?" JP asked.

Just when they thought they couldn't go any faster, the elevator finally began slowing down.

Slowing, slowing, slowing.

"The roof," Mars said as the elevator came to a stop.

As they stepped off the elevator and the doors closed behind them, they felt the ground shudder. There was shaking everywhere around them. It seemed like the air was shaking along with the building.

"Why does it keep shaking like that?" JP asked. "If we're in the middle of an earthquake, I want to know!"

"Droney?" Toothpick asked. "Was that an earthquake?"

Droney was not able to confirm. "Lemon, strawberry, or orange soda?" it chirped.

"What?" Toothpick said, surprised.

"Must be a glitch," said Mars. "That's why drones aren't allowed in the elevators. The speed jumbles their circuits."

"I think they jumbled mine," Caddie said, her hand on her stomach.

"Come this way, gentle people," Mars pressed them.

"Gentle people?" JP snorted. "I think we've entered the twilight zone."

Toothpick was looking at Droney, bemused. "Sorry, I guess that elevator malfunctioned your software, D. I'll take a look."

By now the sun was starting to sink in the sky, casting long orange streaks of light across the sound. The outlines of fishing boats dotted the horizon, and in the distance, the crown of Mount Rainier jutted out from a ring of clouds. It was a breathtaking view. Caddie stood for a moment, her heart beating fast. "Look," she called, pointing.

"Exactly," Mars said. "Everyone stop to look at the amazing view." He shepherded the three of them to the railing. "Have you ever seen anything like it in your life?" His eyes flickered down momentarily to look over the railing. "You wouldn't be able to see this from Port Elizabeth, would you? Only here, way high up on the roof of Pruitt Prep."

Toothpick was the first one to notice the drop. "It's pretty steep, isn't it?" he asked.

"Yes. Yes, it is." Mars let out his breath. "And I'm sorry, guys, but I have to do this."

Before anyone could say anything, they felt Mars's hands on their backs, pushing hard: first Toothpick, then JP and Caddie at the same time. "No . . . Mars!" Their voices pierced the air as they fell, tumbling from the rooftop toward the earth.

## 26

# ESCAPE HATCH

**T**hen the ground met them sooner than anyone expected. There was a thump as the four of them fell onto a ledge jutting out from under the roof.

Caddie lay for a moment in a daze.

"Am I dead?" JP asked. "Am I dreaming?"

"No, we just fell less than two feet," Toothpick said. "This ledge broke our fall."

Mars who had jumped after them, rushed over. "I'm so sorry, guys. It's me in the flesh. This is the only place where there's no camera."

"You *planned* this?" JP said. "Dude!"

Caddie looked at Mars in awe. All his thoughts were coming back, as if the doors that had been closed were now open. They were good ones: *I'm so happy to see you guys; I would never do anything to hurt you; I'm glad you're OK; we're a team forever!*

"You've never done that before, Mars!" she said.

"You mean pushed your friends off the roof to save them?" JP asked. "Well, I've never been a human slingshot, either. Group hug, guys!"

Everyone laughed as they leaned in, happy and relieved. For a few moments, everyone was talking at the same time, sharing what had happened so far while Toothpick opened Droney up and reset his circuits.

"How come I can read your thoughts now and I couldn't before?" Caddie asked, then flushed. "I missed you too, Mars."

"Mind training," Mars said. "It's the first thing they teach you here. You concentrate on one object, like the school building, and that blocks out all your thoughts. We have to go through all these training modules."

"Training for what?" Toothpick asked.

"Not sure, Pick," Mars said. "But mind training was useful. I didn't want you to read my mind, Caddie, and figure everything out."

"What happened in the parking lot, Mars?" JP said. "You never said."

"I happened!" From one of the windows, Jonas crawled out onto the ledge. "First the dudes wearing the white suits came for me at school. Then I went back with them, and we got ole Mars."

"Jonas! You're here," Caddie said. "And you're normal."

"Ha ha," Jonas said. "Sorry, guys. That was Mars's idea. When we saw you in the surveillance cameras, he decided we should pretend we didn't know why you were here and block our thoughts. Otherwise Pruitt would be onto our plan."

"What plan?" Toothpick said.

"To infiltrate Pruitt Prep and find Aurora," Mars said. "What else?"

"Did you find her, Mars?" JP asked. "Or LIL?"

He shook his head. "I didn't hear back from Lost in London. I don't have my phone with me. And I haven't found Aurora, either. At least not yet. But there are so many kids here, guys. You remember the flyers? I recognize some of them."

"Those *are* the missing kids, then!" Caddie said. "But how did they get here?"

"Were they abducted? Did Oliver Pruitt lure them?" JP asked.

"And why do they look so . . . happy?" Caddie wondered. "They don't act like they were kidnapped."

"They *are* happy," Mars said. "Wouldn't you be if you got to be here but you didn't need to take the GIFT? I can't figure it out, but it's like they bypassed the test and now they're here, training for something big. Not sure what. No one says. But there are literally hundreds and hundreds of kids from all over the world. And I'm sure Aurora is one of them."

"Then where is she?" JP asked. "Have you seen her, Jonas?"

He shook his head. "The White Suits have been keeping an eye on me," Jonas said. "I can go most places, but I can't talk to the kids."

"Neither can I," Mars said. "And there's one wing of the building that's heavily guarded—they won't let me go there. But now that you guys are here, we're going to try. Because why do you think they don't want me there?"

"'Cause Aurora is there," Toothpick said. "Good thinking, Mars. So how do we get in?"

"I know most of the access codes," Jonas offered. "They've put me in training the whole time. Flight simulators, combat training, coding, hacking, virtual-reality terrain exploration. Nobody is telling me why, but I guess they think I'm good at that stuff." He shrugged good-naturedly. "And yeah, I guess I am. But I can help you, Mars, with the codes, if there's a door you need opened."

"Caddie, can you sense where Aurora is?" Mars asked.

"I'll try, but I've never been good with her," she said.

"Most people aren't," JP said. "And if you need anyone or anything busted, I can do that."

"Droney's fixed now so he can help with layout,"

Toothpick said. "Including the secret corridors. Right, Droney?"

"Affirmative," Droney responded.

Mars blinked. "I swear, your drone even sounds like you, Pick. All right, guys, let's go!"

One by one, the five of them crawled back through the window Jonas had left open.

Once everyone was inside, Mars paused for a moment to regard Toothpick's drone. "Let's see what you can do, Droney. I'm trying to access the west wing auxiliary chamber. Any chance you know how to get there quick?"

Droney clicked and whirred. "I can show you the way," it said. "Follow me."

All of a sudden it clicked rapidly several times.

"Why is he doing that, Pick?" Jonas asked. "I thought he was fixed."

"He is," Toothpick said. "That's the sound Droney makes when he's making a system alert."

"System alert?" Caddie asked.

"Yeah. Like, danger ahead," Toothpick said.

They looked down the dark hallway where Droney was hovering a few feet ahead of them. Should they turn back or keep going?

"Who's in?" Mars finally asked. "We can't stop now."

"Geez, Mars, do you need to even ask?" JP asked.

Droney clicked.

"Droney says he will lead us," Toothpick said.

"Caddie?" Mars asked.

Caddie could feel everyone's thoughts waiting for her approval, too. It was strange how things had changed in a few days. Mars had always been the leader before he disappeared. Now . . . was she one, too? "Since when has danger stopped us?" she said.

As they continued, JP whispered, "It sure does feel good to be following one of your stupid plans again, Mars."

"My stupid plan?" Mars asked. "What about slingshotting you into the school?"

"That was stupider," Caddie said. "But it worked." She frowned. A headache was starting to grow. She hadn't had one since the day Mars disappeared. It surprised her now, the sudden intensity of it. She wondered if she should say anything or wait until she knew more.

"Great minds think alike, Cads," Mars said.

"I'll say," she said. The pain was jabbing at her. It was getting hard to ignore. "Mars . . ." Her voice came out as a whisper. The headache was getting stronger. Like the one she'd had at the assembly. No. Actually, this was worse. "Mars . . ." she tried again.

Mars hadn't noticed yet. They had reached an intersection of hallways, and he wasn't sure where they were anymore. Meanwhile, Droney was clicking and whirring like crazy.

"Caddie, are you OK?" JP asked suddenly.

"My head," she said weakly.

"Lean on me, Cads," JP said. "Something's wrong with Caddie."

"Droney, too," Toothpick said. "He's on hyper-alert. Something is seriously—" He stopped.

Before he could finish, an entire wall slid open before them. Then came a deafening roar.

"It's that's thing!" JP shouted.

In the hallway, the howling creature seemed even larger than before. Its legs were covered in thick fur and its multiple eyes bore down on them like a spider looks at its prey before striking.

Jonas leaped forward. "Let's see if my combat training helped!"

"Jonas, no!" Caddie called out.

With one swift thrust, the creature batted Jonas out of the way, sending him crashing into a wall. He fell into a heap on the ground.

"Jonas!" JP exclaimed. "I'm coming for you!"

"Nobody move!" The voice was sharp and familiar. The creature instantly retreated as golf-ball-size pellets of food were hurled its way and it commenced eating ravenously.

Dazed, the kids turned around toward the familiar voice.

"Sorry—someone let Muffin out of the room before feeding her," he said.

Standing a few feet away was a man in a white suit and dark-framed glasses, wearing an impenetrable smile. It was Mr. Q.

# 27
# TOO VALUABLE TO LOSE

**M**r. Q, what are you doing here?" asked Mars.

"And that wolf-spider's name is Muffin?" JP asked incredulously.

"She's actually genetically related to a microscopic tardigrade," Mr. Q said. He walked a few paces toward Muffin, who was still devouring her pellets. "Only much larger. Plus, she's been crossbred with a wolf for agility and strength. Which means she's got amazing survival skills, JP."

"Yeah, like for what?" JP asked hotly.

"Oh," Mr. Q said archly. "Everything."

Muffin let out a burp.

"You still haven't said why you're here," Mars said. "You're always showing up when somebody's in trouble. Maybe you're the reason we're in trouble in the first place."

"It's because you work here, don't you, Mr. Q?" Caddie

demanded. "That's why you've been following us. You work for Pruitt!"

At this, the tardigrade rose to her full height and emitted a piercing yowl.

Caddie felt herself wanting to shrink back, but she stood her ground.

Mr. Q held his hands up to soothe Muffin. "There, there."

"You mean you're on Pruitt's side?" JP sputtered. "And here I thought you were cool, like the only grown-up who was looking out for us."

"All those times in detention, you were bringing us cookies," Toothpick said, "and you said we were good kids? You were playing us."

"Listen, everyone. It's complicated," Mr. Q said. "I was looking out for you. But it's bigger than you think." He turned to Mars. "I really thought you had me figured on the boat that night."

"I knew something was up with you," Mars said. "I don't get it. What do you want from us? Why bring me here? And where is Aurora? No one ever answers that."

From down the hallway came a groan.

"Guys," JP said. "I think Jonas is really hurt."

Jonas was struggling to turn over. "That was a doozy," he murmured.

"He'll be OK," said Mr. Q. He reached for the wall and pressed some buttons on a keypad, which seemed to be attached to an intercom. "Hi. Send over a team to Hallway 2C. We've got a student down."

Within a minute, two medics in white suits arrived with a first-aid kit and a stretcher.

"Take our pal Jonas down to infirmary," Mr. Q told them. "Get him fixed up."

"You got it, sir," said one of the medics.

Caddie looked on in dismay.

"So you're working with the White Suits?" she asked. "Unbelievable."

"No, Caddie," Mr. Q said. "They work for me. And for Oliver, of course."

The medics laid out the stretcher. "On the count of three," one of them said to the other.

"Don't touch him," JP said angrily.

"Easy, JP," Mr. Q said. "We're not going to hurt Jonas; we're going to heal him. He's too valuable to lose."

"Too valuable to lose," Caddie murmured. Her attention had shifted to the tardigrade. She was still immense, fully armored, and scary, but in her multiple eyes, Caddie sensed an intelligence and purpose. The tardigrade was watching her, too.

Mr. Q noticed this soundless exchange. "I think Muffin likes you, Caddie," he said wryly. "And by the way, you're all too valuable to lose. Why do you think you're here? You, Mars, Toothpick, JP, and Jonas? You might have noticed by now that you have special powers that get dialed up on Gale Island. That's by design. This island was made to bring out the best in everyone."

"But why, Mr. Q?" Mars asked. "What does Oliver want with all of us?"

By now the two medics had lifted Jonas off the ground and were slowly carrying him down the hall. "We're getting to that, Mars," Mr. Q said. He pressed another button on the wall, and a door opened to reveal a room. "Jonas is going down to the infirmary, and Muffin wants you to wait in there."

"Wait?" Caddie asked. "Wait for what?"

"We're not going inside any room," JP huffed, "not until—" Muffin lunged, and JP let out an uncharacteristic shriek. "Call off your pet spider," JP said fiercely. "Or I can't promise what I'll do next."

"JP," Mars said. "It's OK. I don't think we have a choice."

"Mars is right," Caddie said.

The four of them crossed the threshold into the room.

"Where *are* we?" Mars wondered. "I've never seen this place."

One whole wall of the room was dedicated to computer screens and consoles that displayed various satellite images of Earth, Seattle, and the Port Elizabeth area, each view labeled underneath. There was a row of padded chairs and overhead monitors, and mechanical arms attached to a central station with tiny lights that flashed and beeped.

"It looks like we're inside a control center," Toothpick said. He stared at one of the screens. "Look, that's a Doppler radar of the weather in Seattle. Droney, do you know what this room is used for?"

"Identity and function of this room has been designated confidential," Droney reported. "Cannot confirm."

"Don't worry, kids," Mr. Q said as the door closed behind them. "Someone will be here soon to answer your questions."

∩

**When Mars was seven, it snowed on his birthday. As a baby** in India, he'd never encountered snow, and when he and his mother moved to Port Elizabeth, it was rare for snow to fall in the Puget Sound area. Then on the morning of his seventh birthday, Mars looked out the window and saw his world covered in white, the soft snow covering streets and lawns, the tops of trees and roofs and cars. It snowed two inches that day, and the Seattle area came to a grinding halt. Cars skidded, schools closed, and Saira Patel stayed home from work, looking out from the living room curtains in exasperation and wonder over this white stuff that could cause such havoc. But it was Mars's birthday, so they spent the day drinking hot chocolate and baking spicy samosas in the oven and opening Mars's two presents. One was a children's telescope from Saira, small enough that Mars could set it up himself. He had been begging for one. "I want to see the planets, Mamaji," he told her. "I want to see the stars." The other present had come by special delivery. The courier had trudged through the two inches of snow and handed the brown paper parcel to Mars. Excited, Mars tore apart the paper and held up the toy rocket in the air. "Mamaji!" he exclaimed. And Saira responded quietly, "It was not I who sent it."

The rest of the day, Mars kept looking out the window, not at the snow, but who might walk across it and leave tracks on top of the wondrous snow. If it could snow on his birthday, then other miracles could happen, too. All day he waited, and Saira watched him until she could no longer bear it and said, "Come!" And they went outside, tromping in the snow, throwing snowballs, kicking up the white flakes with their sneakers (neither of them owned snow boots). They didn't talk about the toy rocket or who had sent it. That night, Mars looked out the window at the darkened street, where the snow lay. "Good night, Papaji," he whispered, and he went to bed with the toy rocket next to him, where it would continue to be every night from then on. The next day the snow had melted away.

∩

**For Mars, going with his friends into the windowless room** of Hallway 2C was like the morning he'd woken up after his seventh birthday and found the snow gone. When he was seven, he had been certain his father would come walking across the snow. And when he'd reunited with his friends today at Pruitt Prep, he'd been so sure they would find Aurora and bring her home. And yet here they were, trapped in this odd room, no closer to finding the truth.

"Is everyone OK?" asked Caddie. "JP, stop blaming yourself. I can tell what you're thinking, and you're wrong: you could NOT take down an armored, hybridized tardigrade."

"It was just a large spider, Caddie," JP muttered. "I squash spiders in my house all the time."

"I catch and release them into the wild," Toothpick said. "It's important to preserve biodiversity."

"Listen, Muffin isn't a spider; she's a huge tardigrade, genetically crossbred with a wolf!" Caddie pointed out. "Look what happened to Jonas."

"And that's my fault," Mars mumbled. "What if Jonas doesn't get better?"

"He'll be all right, Mars," Caddie said gently. "I can feel it." She watched him. She had felt his memories, the first snowfall, the toy rocket on his bed, and now the disappointment stirring in him. "Mars, it's going to be OK."

"I'm sorry, guys," Mars said. "I—I don't know what to do. I think they've got us."

"We can still win," Toothpick said.

"What are you talking about, Pick?" JP asked glumly. "If it's not obvious, us being locked up in a room with a giant spider outside guarding us is what LOSING looks like."

"You don't understand," Toothpick said. "When I reprogrammed Droney, I set him to record everything in Pruitt Prep: the missing kids, the tardigrade, what Mr. Q said about the island. Everything. We've got him on all of it. And this room looks important, too. Droney has made a video recording of it. Now I can use a satellite link to send a composite video to Epica. She can broadcast it to the world. It can go viral, just like Mars's video did."

Around them the lights flickered, and the building shook violently again.

"Whoa," JP said, bracing themself against one of the padded chairs.

An image shimmered before them. Even as a hologram, Oliver Pruitt cut an impressive figure. Gone were the Hawaiian shirt, lei, and bamboo hat he'd sported on the Gale Island ferry. This Oliver Pruitt was lean, powerful, his dark hair cropped short, and he was wearing a fitted white jumpsuit that outlined his tall, imposing body.

"I must warn you, Mr. Lee," Oliver said, "if you go public like that, you will never see your friends again."

# 28
## DECISIONS, DECISIONS

**P**ruitt!" JP said. "Why am I not surprised?"

"It's another hologram," Caddie said. "And I can't read holograms." She watched as the hologram of Oliver strode across the floor. It was amazing how lifelike it looked. She could even see the flare of his nostrils and the small creases in his jumpsuit.

Droney clicked. "A hologram is a 3D recording of an image using a light field."

"Thanks, Droney. We get it; we see him," JP said. "The question is how do we get rid of him?"

"You like to make jokes, don't you, JP?" Oliver's voice sounded slightly amused. "But this is no joking matter. We have much work to do."

"You know what, Oliver Pruitt?" Mars shouted. "Maybe we're tired of all your games. There's only one reason we're here in your fancy school, and that's to find Aurora. So if you'll just—"

"Mars, Mars," Oliver interrupted. "You're working yourself up. You didn't come here by accident. Nor did your friends. Do you want to know *why* I brought you extraordinary young people to my school? Even you, JP, the handful that you are?"

"Want to get another 'handful' while I unplug you again, Pruitt?" JP threatened. They looked around the room for the power source but couldn't find it. Oliver was getting projected some other way.

Mars had had enough. "Where's Aurora?" he demanded. "What do you want from us?"

"I can give you answers," Oliver said. "But first, I need you each to make a choice of your own free will."

This was unexpected. Everyone stopped to consider Oliver Pruitt's words.

Meanwhile, the floor and walls began to shake.

"There it goes again," said JP.

"Why does the building keep shaking so much?" asked Toothpick.

Oliver's amused expression was gone. He was looking at them seriously. "That shaking you feel is our school wall retracting. Not only is our titanium wall twenty feet tall and as impregnable as Gibraltar, it's fully retractable and undetectable once in the ground. Why am I telling you that? Because right now, you can all choose to leave Pruitt Prep. No one is stopping you. The doors will be open, the wall will be down, and the ferry will be waiting when you get to the shore. Is that correct, Mr. Q?"

Mr. Q, who was standing near the door, nodded. "That's right, kids," he said.

Oliver smiled, and when he did, Caddie was surprised by how his whole demeanor changed. He looked so kind! So safe and trustworthy, like someone who would hold your hand when you crossed the street. But Caddie knew Oliver was not someone she could trust.

"What's the catch?" Mars asked.

"The catch is," Oliver said, "you have to leave here without answers."

"That's not bad," JP said.

"And without Jonas and Aurora."

"Oh," JP said. "That's not so good."

"And if we stay?" Mars asked.

"If you stay, then you will know everything. And I mean *everything*. You'll know about my school, about the kids who build and create here, about the wondrous projects that will take us into the next century. But you will never go back home again."

"Never?" Mars asked. "I don't understand."

"What about our parents?" Toothpick asked.

"They'll be well taken care of," Oliver said. "But you're right: you won't be with them."

For a moment, everyone was quiet, letting the words sink in.

Toothpick started pacing. "But I can't fall asleep if my mom and dad don't tuck me in," he said. Next to him, Droney clicked.

"JP?" Oliver asked next. "What's your answer?"

JP was twisting the end of their scarf nervously. "My dad's birthday is next month. He saved up for tickets for us to see the Seahawks play. And that's only 'cause of me. He'd rather go to his classics conference or something, but then I kept bugging him and . . ." JP swallowed. "Couldn't we put it off by a few weeks?"

"I'm afraid not, JP," Oliver said. "Caddie? How about you? Are you ready to make the choice? I can't read your mind, you know."

Caddie looked at Mars. What was Mars feeling? Anguish at the idea of leaving his mom. Guilt because of Aurora. Of course he would feel that way, responsible for Aurora, who wasn't even here. Is that what she had chosen? Never to come back?

"Do we at least get to say goodbye?" Caddie asked. "I mean, my parents aren't easy to get along with, but they are my parents, you know." By now her mom would have discovered Caddie's empty room. What would her mom say? What would she do if she never saw Caddie again? Sure, she was ready to send her daughter off to boarding school, and Pruitt Prep was kind of a boarding school . . . but forever?

"Mr. Pruitt, why can't our parents come visit us here?" Mars asked. "Why are you doing this? Why are you making us choose?"

"I can't tell you why," Oliver said softly. "Not until you've made the choice."

He stood before them, shimmering, but it was undeniable in his face: he seemed to feel their sadness, too. Could it be possible that Oliver wasn't so bad after all? Caddie considered the man's wealth and fortune, his fame and ambition. Seemed like a lonely life, too. What was it that Oliver wanted? And what could he possibly want from them?

"Choose quickly, please," Oliver urged. "We haven't got much time."

"I said I'd find Aurora wherever she is," Mars said softly. "And a promise is a promise."

Caddie stared at him. "But you didn't promise *her*, Mars! You promised yourself—that's not the same thing!"

"But that isn't what Mars thinks, is it?" Oliver Pruitt asked. He turned to Mr. Q. "Oh yes, can we take care of that one last thing?"

Mr. Q walked over to them with a handset. "The connection's ready," he said to Oliver.

"Take the handset," Oliver said to Mars. "Your mother is on the line."

What was going on? Caddie and JP exchanged looks. Was Mars agreeing to Oliver's terrible proposition? Caddie had to stop him. But Mars was already on the phone.

"Mars?" Saira Patel's voice crackled across the line on speakerphone.

"Hello, Ma?" Mars said back.

"Is that you? Are you all right?" Her voice was filled with concern. "When you didn't come back, I didn't know what to think."

Caddie, Toothpick, and JP tried to look like they weren't listening in. Oliver stood waiting nearby, his face unreadable, but everyone could tell he was hearing every word, too.

Behind Oliver, Mr. Q was fiddling with one of the consoles that displayed a view of the school grounds. Caddie watched absently until she realized what she was seeing. The titanium walls were gone! Oliver was right. They had disappeared, leaving an open path to the woods.

*And freedom*, she thought.

"I'm sorry I ran away, Mamaji," Mars was saying, his voice laden with guilt.

"I know, Mars. And I know why you're there—I knew one day it would happen. It is meant to be because you're special. That's why Oliver chose you. He thought you were . . . special, too."

"I guess so." Mars was doubtful. Was he really that special?

*Yes!* Caddie wanted to shout across the room. She wanted to shout so many things. She wanted to stop this crazy decision! But Mars's mom kept talking, her voice shaking in the windowless room.

"I always knew," Saira said, "you have a great destiny. Remember that, no matter what you learn about anyone . . . including me. I'm proud of you, Mars."

"I love you, Ma," Mars said softly.

Caddie was feeling desperate. She couldn't let Mars make this mistake. How could his mom let him stay here with Oliver Pruitt? Didn't she understand that Mars was never coming home?

"I love you, too," Saira said like she was holding back tears. "Remember the snow, beta. Always remember the snow. I'll see you in the stars."

"I'll see you in the stars," Mars whispered.

"Mars, wait . . ." Caddie started.

Saira Patel's voice was abruptly cut off.

"Ma?" Mars said, then repeated her name but there was no response.

"I'm so sorry, Mars," Oliver said. "We must have lost the connection. I know that was difficult for you."

Mr. Q took the handset from Mars. "Who's next?" he asked.

The rest of them looked back at him in dread.

"Mr. Q?" Mars said in a small voice. "I need to talk to you."

The two of them walked away to a corner.

"What are they saying?" JP asked, straining to hear.

"I can't hear them," Toothpick said.

"Caddie, what's going on? What are you getting?" JP asked.

Caddie was frowning in concentration. Then a moment later, she gasped. "Mars, no!"

"What, Caddie?" JP said. "What's he saying?"

"Are you sure?" Mr. Q asked, walking Mars back to the group.

"Yeah, I'm sure," Mars said. His face was resolute.

"Oliver?" Mr. Q asked him expectantly.

"What? What?" JP asked. "No one's telling me anything."

"He said to take him and make the rest of us leave," burst Caddie. "Mars? You can't. What about us?"

"OK, then," Oliver said. "It's a deal."

"Mars?" JP said, stunned. "You made a deal . . . with these liars?"

The door opened and a swarm of White Suits spilled in, two for every kid.

"What's going on?" JP cried. "Hey! Get your hands off me!"

"I'm sorry, guys," Mars said.

"Mars, you can't send us away," Caddie pleaded.

"You're sending us away?" JP yelled. "I hate you, Oliver Pruitt! You're splitting us up."

"JP, I ruined your lives," Mars said. "Got you more detention and almost thrown out of school for good. I can't ask you to stay away from your families forever."

"But Mars," Toothpick said. "We're a team."

"We'll always be a team, Pick," Mars said to him. "Whether we're together or not. Goodbye, buddy. You're the smartest person I've ever met. And I've met Oliver Pruitt."

"Mars," Toothpick said, but he could not think what to say next. He could not think how to stop Mars.

"My parents will get over it, Mars," JP sputtered. "Let me stay, too. I can protect you."

Mars patted JP on the shoulder. "I'm sorry, JP. Take care of these guys, OK?"

"Mars, please don't do this," Caddie implored.

"I'm going to miss you, Caddie," he said. "You're the best person I know. I hope you can tell what I'm thinking." He gave her a wavering smile.

"Yes. I hear it," Caddie whispered. "Me, too."

"Come on, guys, time to go," Mr. Q said, signaling to the White Suits.

The kids tried to pull away, but there were too many White Suits forcing them out of the room. Caddie's last view of Mars was of him standing next to Oliver Pruitt—a brave young person and a cold-hearted beast.

**"OK, Mr. Pruitt," Mars said to the hologram. "Now you've** got me. So what gives?"

Mars tried to sound tough, but meanwhile he was wondering if he had just made the biggest mistake of his life. First, that call with his mother where he had to say goodbye forever, then watching his friends get dragged out while he was stuck inside this gadget room with someone who wasn't even real, just a stupid light beam. What if that's all Oliver Pruitt ever was? A light beam? A trick of the eye? A joke?

"Mars, you have been very brave," Oliver said. "You are everything I hoped you'd be."

"Well, you're not," Mars said. "Actually you're the opposite."

Oliver laughed. "You certainly don't mince words. Look, Mars, I'm not the bad guy. I'm not here to tie you up and throw you to the wolves. But first I needed to know that you were up to the task. I needed to know you have what it takes."

"I don't get it," Mars said.

"I'm here to show you a different way. I see how it's

turning out: our world is crumbling, and no one is doing anything about it. It's time for a new future, Mars, and believe or not, *kids* are going to lead the way."

For a second, Mars felt himself stirring. This sounded like the old Oliver Pruitt talking, the one Mars used to believe in, the one who made anything sound possible. Infinite Ping-Pong, artificial plants, beating hearts forever. "What do you mean? What's going happen?"

Behind him, Mr. Q had been typing into a console. Now he was done, and he said to Oliver, "Ready. All systems check."

"Excellent," Oliver said. "You may go."

"Mr. Q?" Mars called out as his teacher walked toward the door. "You're leaving me here?"

Mr. Q smiled faintly. "Actually, I think you're the one who's doing the leaving," he said before closing the door behind him.

"Huh?"

"Mars, I need you to take a seat in the orange chair right now," Oliver said.

"I'm so confused," Mars said. "Mr. Q says I'm leaving, and you're telling me to sit down."

"Listen to what I tell you. Remember, you're here to find Aurora."

Hearing Aurora's name was like a jolt. Mars looked at

the big orange chair, which was more like a sleeping pod bolted to the ground. For a moment he contemplated opening the room door and leaving just like Mr. Q had. Maybe the school doors were still open, the ferry still docked, his friends still waiting on the other side. But they were safe. It was Aurora who was gone. He climbed into the giant chair. Around him the room had started to hum.

*"Unit has been pressurized,"* an automated woman's voice announced.

"Good," Oliver said to Mars. "Sit back; get comfortable. I know these choices haven't been easy, Mars, but life is filled with difficult choices. And where you're going, there will be many more."

"Where I'm going? What's going on? Where's Aurora? Where are you?"

The mechanical arms next to Mars stirred to life. Swiftly they strapped him in, with buckles clamping around his ankles and wrists.

"Hey! Stop! Why am I being strapped in like this?" Mars wriggled, surprised by the sudden movement of the mechanical arms.

"For your own safety, of course," Oliver called out.

*"Launch sequence activated,"* a second automated voice announced overhead. *"Countdown commences."*

Oliver's hologram abruptly flickered off, but his voice

continued to boom across the speakers in the room. *"Five, four, three . . ."* He was counting along with the automated voice.

Around him, Mars's world started to shake. But this time the shaking didn't stop. There was a giant roar, and Mars felt as if the room was being wrenched from the ground.

"Two . . . one," Oliver finished.

*"Liftoff. Launch Pad Three."*

A force unlike anything Mars had ever felt in his life seemed to be sucking him up, pulling him from the inside and the outside. Was he dying? Was he being reborn?

"Mars, when you look back at this moment," Oliver's voice cut through, strangely tender, "you'll know *this* was when your life changed. You'll realize this was the start of your destiny. Press the red button on your right and look out the window. Then you'll see what I mean."

Window? What window? Mars reached mutely for the button. Immediately the ceiling opened up, revealing a world receding fast. Gone were the titanium walls and even the twin towers of Pruitt Prep, leaving nothing behind but an open field. The shores of Gale Island grew faint, as the shining lights of Seattle became dots along the ocean, and then nothing.

Mars found words at last. "The school is flying? We're in the air?"

"Not for long," Oliver said. "You're about to break through Earth's atmosphere."

"The Earth? Pruitt Prep . . ." Mars's mind was agog. "Pruitt Prep is a spaceship?"

"We call it a spacecraft," Oliver said. "The towers and wall were built to retract, allowing our state-of-the-art rocket to enter space. That's why I wasn't there last time you came."

"But . . . but," Mars sputtered, losing his grip on both reality and Earth. "Where's Aurora?"

"She's right here with me," Oliver said. "Say hi, Aurora."

Through the speakers a familiar voice rang. "Mars? Is that you, Mars?"

"We're signing off," Oliver called out. "Sit back and say goodbye to Earth, my friend. I can't wait to see you. It seems I've been waiting my whole life for the day I'll see you here . . . on Mars."

∩

**As Mars traveled in space, he traveled backward and for-**ward in time. He remembered the playground with Caddie, where they built sandcastles with plastic buckets and twigs; he remembered JP's sparkly scarf fluttering in the wind; he remembered Aurora's spiky wristbands and missing father and the promise he'd made to her standing outside the back door; he remembered Toothpick's survival matches and Jonas's Mariners cap. He remembered his mom's jingly bangles and throaty laugh. And he remembered the snow. It would be months and months before he reached his destination. He would be six months older but a lifetime older, too. And nothing would ever be the same again when the hatch finally opened and Mars emerged, setting foot on frozen-solid red ground.

# FROM THE PODCAST

Listeners, what would you do to save yourself?
What would you do to save your friends?
What you would do tells me what kind of person you are.

Sometimes our future is racing toward us.
Sometimes we're the ones hurtling
toward it at breakneck speed.

Whatever your destiny may be, be brave, be bold.
Be the beam of light that saves us all.

To the stars!

**2.3 mil Comments** ⊗

staryoda    12 min ago
we don't need the GIFT to do all those things

oreocookies    10 min ago
someone told me Pruitt Prep is broke

allie_j    5 min ago
Then can I get in?? I still <3 Pruitt Prep

galaxygenius   4 min ago
I heard Mars is going to be in charge

epica_is_epic   3 min ago
peace out mars

godzilla   3 min ago
peace out mars

neptunebaby   3 min ago
peace out mars

lostinlondon   1 min ago
Ad astra Mars and godspeed

# ACKNOWLEDGMENTS

**It has been a gift to live and breathe the world of Mars Patel.** I thank Benjamin Strouse, Chris Tarry, David Kreizman, Jenny Turner Hall, and the entire cast and crew who worked so hard to create the original podcast series of *The Unexplainable Disappearance of Mars Patel*. Thank you for allowing me to be part of the magic by putting this story down on paper.

Thank you to Marietta Zacker for expertly shepherding this project from the very beginning, and to Steven Malk for all his guidance and support, and for knowing that working on Mars Patel would be perfect for me. I couldn't ask for a better team!

And thank you to Susan Van Metre, my esteemed editor! I'm beyond happy and grateful for your excellent editorial eye, for knowing where I needed to go deeper and where to pull back, and how to always keep sight of my characters.

And yay for more meals, more ideas, more sparkle, and more insight I got to experience with you. You're out of this world! Thank you to the rest of the Walker Books team, including Maria Middleton, Maya Myers, and Maggie Deslaurier for making sure this book turned out perfectly and beautifully in every possible way.

Thanks to one of my favorite people in the world, Sasha Ericksen, and to her family for inviting me to stay in their beautiful home. What better way to return to Washington State than to spend it there, looking out quietly onto the water? A special shout-out to Ben, who spent the day with us going by ferry to Seattle and wandering around Pike Place Market. Hanging out with him gave me much inspiration for Port Elizabeth and the young people living there.

Thank you to Emmett Donovan, who read over chapters and gave me such astute and thoughtful feedback. We should all be so lucky to have as careful and generous a reader as Emmett.

Lastly, thank you to my cherished family, Meera, Keerthana, and Suresh. You are all the reason why I can and do write. You are my sun, moon, and all the planets. Special gratitude to Meera for her intelligence and wit, and for keeping my writing real. To the stars!

Enjoy this sneak peek at

# THE INTERPLANETARY EXPEDITION OF

# MARS PATEL

the second book in
the MARS PATEL series.

Hey, podcast listeners, Oliver Pruitt here.
Welcome to a different journey!

With all great adventure comes great risk,
but I believe in the future I'm building,
especially with Mars Patel on the way!

Happy LANDING, but do be careful.
That first step is a doozy . . .

To the stars!

**1124 Comments** ⊗

staryoda    38 min ago
**did OP kidnap mars??**

allie_j    33 min ago
**maybe OP & Mars r the same person**

galaxygenius    26 min ago

no way mars is human OP is not

lostinlondon    15 min ago

OP is human and he's saving your idiot planet

he's saving us all

# 1
## WELCOME TO ZERO GRAVITY

When Mars dreamed of traveling to distant planets, vomit wasn't the first thing that came to mind. But here he was hurtling through space on the *Pruitt 3*, hurling into a barf bag.

"Mars, say goodbye to Earth! You are about to go on the adventure of your life!" crowed Oliver Pruitt, the billionaire inventor who had orchestrated this journey on his own spaceship. Of course, he wasn't *actually* in the cockpit. Only a hologram version of him stood there. But that didn't stop the man from gushing virtually from his control center millions of miles away. "Go on, float around," Oliver called out as Mars turned green. "Welcome to zero gravity!"

Just a few minutes ago, after leaving Earth, Mars had unbuckled his harness and felt himself free-floating inside the walls of the cockpit, somersaulting and pinwheeling his way through the cabin. First he was right side up, then he was upside down until his limbs felt like clouds, and the universe zoomed by outside in a veil of darkness. Was this really happening to him? Was he really on a spaceship headed to the planet Mars?

Meanwhile, Oliver Pruitt watched, looking sharp in his maroon space suit. Mars wasn't even sure when Oliver had changed. Back on Earth, he had appeared to Mars and his friends in a muted white flight suit. Now Mars's friends and his mom were left behind, maybe forever. It had been twelve minutes since liftoff, but to Mars, it felt like a lifetime. He needed to know where Aurora was, and why Oliver had led him to outer space, far from everyone Mars loved.

But first Mars had other problems. He heaved into the paper bag.

"I think I just barfed up a lung," he said weakly.

"Nothing like traveling through space for the first time! What you're feeling, Mars, is motion sickness as your body adjusts to weightlessness. But don't worry. You'll get used it in no time. And then the fun really begins!"

The door to the cockpit burst open.

"Mr. Pruitt, we've got a problem," announced a girl in an orange flight suit who had tumbled into the room. She was small-boned with a slightly upturned nose and a cascade of dark brown curls framing her square face.

Mars stared in disbelief. "You're Lost in London! I mean, you're Julia!" He recognized her immediately from the missing-children flyers he and his friends had found back in Port Elizabeth. But where had she come from? Had she been on the spacecraft the entire time? "When did you get here?" he asked.

Julia rolled her eyes at him but her voice was gentle. "Mars, I didn't *get* here, I've *been* here. But honestly, I don't have time to explain when we're in an emergency. Mr. Pruitt, I need to know if—"

But hologram Oliver Pruitt was fading away.

Julia's eyebrows knitted together. "Mr. Pruitt!" she repeated crossly.

"Sorry, Julia! Have to run! But it sounds like you've got it under control!" Oliver Pruitt was growing fainter and fainter until he was just a shimmer.

"Wait! Don't go!" Mars cried out. "You need to answer my questions. Where's Aurora? What's going to happen to my friends and my mom? And why did you lie to me? Why did you make us go through all of that on Earth?"

"That's a lot of questions," Oliver said wryly.

"I need to know!"

"I had to make sure you were ready for the Red Planet." Oliver now was barely an outline. "Wait until you get here. The Colony will blow your mind!"

"Colony?" Mars repeated. "Is that where Aurora is?"

"There's so much to tell you, Mars. About why I chose you for the mission. Because you are . . ."

The spaceship lurched horribly.

"WARNING: BREACH IMMINENT IN SECTOR C." The announcement rang across the speakers, followed by an alarm.

"Mr. Pruitt!" Julia said again more urgently. But Oliver Pruitt had vanished from the cockpit. "Oh, great! Just what we need. A commander-in-chief who's MIA."

"WARNING: BREACH IMMINENT IN SECTOR C."

The alarm sounded again, and Mars felt like his life was repeating. Wasn't it just a few weeks ago that he and Caddie were inside a janitor closet at school hiding out during a Code Red? Were alarms going to follow him his whole life—even in space?

"Is that warning serious?" Mars asked nervously. "What does it mean?"

Julia had floated to an intercom mounted on the wall and now said loudly into the mic, "We need you on the flight deck—NOW!" Then she turned to Mars. "It means that if we don't do something about that hole in Sector C, we're going to burn up like a marshmallow on an open flame. Which is what I was trying to tell Oliver Pruitt before he vanished on us."

"WARNING: CATASTROPHIC BREACH IN SECTOR C.

CATASTROPHIC BREACH IN SECTOR C. ALL SYSTEMS DISENGAGE IN THREE MINUTES."

"Does that mean we're going to die?" Mars felt his heart thud. Until now it had seemed like things were going well enough. Sure, he'd thought Pruitt Prep was a normal school on Gale Island, until he found out that it was also a spacecraft heading to Mars. And sure, Oliver had tricked him into coming on board, but Mars hadn't expected to die on the man's watch.

Now Oliver was gone. And catastrophe was around the corner.

"It means we have to handle this problem ourselves," Julia said. "That means *you*, Mars."

"But I d-don't—" Mars stuttered in a panic. "I've never been on a spaceship, and I never—"

Julia steeled herself. "I get it. This is all new for you. It's natural to freak out. But I need you to calm down so you can help us not die. You think you can handle that?"

Behind Julia, a panel slid open. A teenage guy in a gray flight suit floated in. His brown eyes were wide-spaced and intelligent, and he looked like he hadn't had a haircut in weeks. "Places, everybody," he said easily. "These interplanetary space shuttles don't fly themselves."

Mars stared at him, agog. Who else was on board this spaceship?

"You really took forever, Orion," Julia said. "We have less than three minutes."

Orion tumbled toward the cockpit and slipped into the pilot seat. He strapped himself in next to Julia, who was already strapped and waiting for him. "I heard, I heard," he said to her. He inputted some numbers into the control panel. "Julia, you handle the throttle."

"Roger that."

Orion turned to Mars. "How about you, Butterfly?" he said evenly.

"Butterfly?" Mars repeated. "Wait, who are you?"

"Mars, Orion, Orion, Mars," Julia said, making quick introductions. "He's the pilot."

"Think you can spin us?" Orion pointed to a wheel mounted on a console behind them.

"I guess," Mars said unsurely.

"That will mean you aren't buckled in, OK?" Orion asked. "So hold on tight, or you're really going to be flying around here like a butterfly. Start turning that wheel. Now!"

The wheel was surprisingly heavy. Mars gripped the handle in both hands, breathing hard as he rotated. "What does this do?" he asked, panting.

"We're turning this craft manually," Orion explained, his eyes on the flight monitor. "I already applied a patch from the service module, using a bot. That ought to hold us. Later, when we get to the space station, we'll repair the breach for real."

"OK." Mars stopped talking as he concentrated all his energy on turning the wheel. Orion was right. It was taking everything to hold on so that Mars wouldn't find himself thrown against the walls of the flight deck.

Meanwhile, Julia and Orion continued steering while Mars kept turning the wheel and announcements blared overhead: low pressurization, acceleration, deceleration, oxygen levels, radiation levels. Then a few minutes later, the announcements stopped. The lights came on in the room. And the spinning stopped. Mars let go of the wheel and floated gratefully to an open chair. Through the monitors, he could see the spacecraft moving forward as Orion finished entering coordinates into the panel.

"Back on autopilot," Orion said. "And on track to reaching Pruitt Space Station at expected arrival time."

"Excellent work, Orion," Julia said. "Of course, you *are* the best pilot at Pruitt Prep."

"Yeah, but you're the one who spotted the breach." Orion stretched back in his chair. "So that just leaves you, Butterfly. Why are you here, again?"

"Why do you keep calling me that?" Mars asked.

"'Cause you look like one, flying around like somebody's gonna eat you."

"No, I don't!" Mars jumped up from his chair so suddenly

that the momentum spun him forward into the monitors. He leaned back, rubbing his sore arm.

"Butterfly!"

"Quit calling me that!"

"Oh, bloody stop, both of you," Julia said. She had clearly had enough. "Orion, you know who he is. He's Mars Patel."

Orion gave a good-natured smile and held his hands up in the universal gesture of backing off. Even though he looked a few years older, it was clear he respected what Julia had to say. "Course. I was just messing with him."

"Just because this is your second trip to Mars," Julia said, "doesn't mean you get to ruffle everyone's feathers."

"I got you," Orion said.

Behind Julia, Mars noticed something strange with one of the monitors. "Hey, why is it dark in Cargo? Is everything OK? Did something break when we were spinning?"

Orion's smile faded. "Nope. It's dark for a reason, Butterfly. Stay out."

"Why?" Mars asked. "Maybe you should check—"

Orion stood up quickly, his feet catapulting him off the ground. "I said, stay out!"

"It's some special delivery Mr. Pruitt put Orion in charge of," Julia said to Mars. "Even I don't know what it is. But boy, does Orion get his shorts bunched up over it.'"

"Why does everything have to be so secretive around here?" Mars grumbled.

"Listen, Butterfly Breath," Orion said. "This ain't no H. G. Wells Middle School. Yeah, Julia and me know all about you and your friends back home. If you guys don't like something, you just break the rules and go to detention. Well, that's not how it works here. You mess up, you DIE."

"I think I can take care of myself," Mars said hotly. He decided to ignore the fact that just a few minutes ago he had been clutching a barf bag.

"Mars, Orion is right," Julia said gravely. "This is a dangerous place. Remember what just happened."

"You mean the breach?" Mars said. "I thought that was an accident and we fixed it."

Julia and Orion glanced at each other. A whole unspoken conversation seemed to flow between them.

"That breach was no accident," Orion said ominously. "That was *sabotage*."

# ABOUT THE AUTHOR

**SHEELA CHARI** is the author of *Finding Mighty*, a Junior Library Guild Selection and Children's Book Council Children's Choice Finalist, and *Vanished*, an APALA Children's Literature Award Honor Book, an Edgar Award nominee for best juvenile mystery, and a *Today* Book Club Selection. She has an MFA from New York University and teaches fiction writing at Mercy College. Sheela Chari lives with her family in New York.

doc